JUDI CURTIN grew up in Cork and now lives in Limerick where she is married with three children. Her 'Alice & Megan' series, as well as *Alice & Megan's Cookbook* and *Eva's Journey*, are all published by The O'Brien Press. With Roisin Meaney, she is the author of *See If I Care*, and she has also written three novels, *Sorry, Walter, From Claire to Here* and *Almost Perfect*. Her books have been translated into Serbian, Portuguese and German.

The 'Alice & Megan' series

Alice Next Door

Alice Again

Don't Ask Alice

Alice in the Middle

Bonjour Alice

Alice & Megan Forever

Alice to the Rescue

Alice & Megan's Cookbook

Other Books

Eva's Journey

Praise for *Alice to the Rescue*

'Always charming, sometimes laugh-out-loud funny, this book about two best friends is a treat' *Irish Independent*

'A touching story about the ways friendship can fix even the most seemingly difficult problems' *CBI Bookfest Guide 2009*

ANA SORA

Alice to the Rescue

Judi Curtin

Illustrations: Woody Fox

THE O'BRIEN PRESS
DUBLIN

First published 2009 by The O'Brien Press Ltd,
12 Terenure Road East, Rathgar, Dublin 6, Ireland.
Tel: +353 1 4923333; Fax: +353 1 4922777
E-mail: books@obrien.ie
Website: www.obrien.ie
Reprinted 2010.

ISBN: 978-1-84717-175-7

A catalogue record for this title is available from the British Library

2 3 4 5 6 7 8
10 11 12 13 14

The O'Brien Press receives

assistance from

Illustrations: Woody Fox
Layout and design: The O'Brien Press Ltd
Printed by CPI Cox and Wyman
The paper in this book is produced using pulp from managed forests.

For Mum and Dad

Many, many thanks to everyone who helped with this book. If you don't know who you are by now, I give up. (But just in case, thanks to: Dan, Annie, Ellen, Brian, Helen, Brenda, Ruth, Emma, Michael, Ivan, Kunak, Sarah and Woody.)

I really appreciate it when people take the trouble to let me know that they are enjoying the 'Alice & Megan' books. Special mention has to go to the enthusiastic letter-writers from Tiermohan NS and the eager e-mailers from The Heath NS. Thank You!

Chapter one

I ate the last spoonful of porridge, and got up from the table to put my bowl into the dishwasher. Mum gave a big long sigh, making her straggly, curly fringe rise up into the air, almost as if it was getting ready to fly off into outer space.

'I'm going to miss you, Megan,' she said.

I gave an even bigger sigh.

'Mum, that is *soooo* pathetic,' I said. 'It's not like I'm going to America for six months. I'm only going to school. It's just up the road, and I'll be home at half past three.'

Mum shook her head impatiently.

'That's not the point, Megan,' she said. 'I've got used to you being around the house during the Christmas holidays. It will be so quiet here when you're gone.'

I didn't answer. Even when I was there, the house was too quiet for me.

I love Christmas. I love opening presents (even home-made ones from my mum). I love the smell of the Christmas tree (but I hate being the one who has to plant it in the garden again when Christmas is over). I love eating the chocolate bars from the selection box my aunt Linda sends me every year (even though she knows it drives my mum crazy). I love being able to stay in my pyjamas for half the day. I love … well, I just love every single thing about Christmas.

But after two weeks of Christmas with my family, I was ready to go back to school. I was ready to go back out into the real world.

'Your second term at secondary school,' Mum was saying in a dreamy kind of voice. 'How did that happen so quickly? I remember when—'

Just then the doorbell rang. I grinned. It's like Alice has some kind of radar that lets her know when I'm in trouble. She always manages to come to the rescue just in time.

'Sorry, Mum,' I said. 'I'd really love to hear what you remember, but some other time, OK?'

'Don't be cheeky, young lady,' said Mum, but she was smiling, so I knew she wasn't cross.

Just then my little sister Rosie appeared in the kitchen. She looked totally sweet in her fleecy pyjamas, with her hair all damp and curly. I felt a bit sorry for her – she just gets to go to playschool in the mornings and then she's stuck at home with Mum all afternoon, eating healthy food and playing educational games.

I bent down and kissed her.

'See you later,' I said.

Then I gave Mum a quick kiss, grabbed my coat and my school-bag and ran out to meet Alice.

*   *   *

Alice and I hugged each other. Then I bent down to stroke Domino, my pet kitten, who had just appeared and was rubbing against my leg with her soft fur. Domino had only strayed into my life a few months earlier, but already it felt like she'd been mine forever.

'Bye, Domino,' I said. 'Be a good girl until I get home.'

Alice rolled her eyes.

'Still talking to animals, I see. Know what, Megan? You badly need to get back to school.'

I laughed.

'Tell me about it,' I said.

I picked Domino up and she wriggled until

she was comfortable in my arms.

'Isn't she the sweetest thing you've ever seen?' I asked.

Alice backed away. I keep forgetting that Alice doesn't like cats very much. I think she's even a bit afraid of Domino, but she's too proud to admit it.

'We're going to be late if we don't get a move on,' said Alice, not answering my question.

I put Domino down, and Alice backed even further away as the little cat slunk past her.

Then Alice and I set off down the road towards school.

'I'm *so* looking forward to seeing everyone again,' said Alice. 'I think I'm even looking forward to seeing Miss Leonard.'

I giggled. Miss Leonard is our Home Economics teacher, and I'm fairly sure she wasn't looking forward to seeing Alice.

'At least that awful Marcus won't be around to

scare you any more,' said Alice.

I didn't answer. Marcus had been in my class until just before Christmas, and he *had* started off being really scary, but in the end I felt sorry for him. Even though he did some bad things, he was nice underneath. I'd never found the right time to tell Alice that, in a funny kind of way, Marcus had been my friend.

'At least you're never going to hear from *him* again,' said Alice.

Once again I didn't reply.

What would Alice say if she knew that Marcus had texted me from his new boarding school only half an hour earlier?

Sometimes things are just too complicated to put into words.

* * *

Before long we were at the usual corner where our friends Grace and Louise were waiting for us.

We all hugged, and then continued on our walk, chatting about the Christmas holidays. Grace had been on a skiing holiday, and made us all laugh as she told us stories about the crazy, but very good-looking, German boy in her skiing class.

Just before we got to school, we met my friend Kellie, and the five of us walked through the school gates together. I wasn't scared like I had been back in September.

I felt brave and happy and ready for a whole new year.

Chapter two

We had assembly first thing, so we all made our way to the big hall. It was kind of fun, waving at people I hadn't seen over the holidays. Everyone was chatting and laughing. The girls were hugging each other, and the boys were pretending to think that was gross. Then the principal, Mrs Kingston, stepped on to the stage, and everyone stood quietly.

'Bet this is going to be totally boring,' whispered Alice with a big sigh. 'What do you think, Meg?'

I didn't reply. Mrs Kingston was *really* strict about talking in assembly. Why was Alice whispering? Did she want to get in trouble on the very first morning?

As usual, Alice was right, though. There was about twenty minutes of boring stuff, and then, at last, Mrs Kingston said something interesting.

'This year, we've decided to try something new,' she began. 'There's a very large range of abilities in your English classes, so we have decided to divide you up based on the results of your Christmas exams. This means that, for English lessons only, you will no longer be taught in your usual class groups, but in the new ones, which are on the lists at the back of the room.'

Everyone immediately turned to look, but turned back again just as quickly when Mrs Kingston let out a sudden loud cry.

'PATIENCE!' she shouted, so loudly that almost everyone, including me, jumped. 'You can all see the lists on your way out, and *not* before then.'

Mrs Kingston went on with loads more boring stuff after that, but I couldn't pay any attention. I love English and had done really well in my Christmas exam, but I couldn't remember how Alice or any of my other friends had done. If they had done well we could all be together for English, which would be totally great. I was too afraid to ask them though, as Mrs Kingston was wearing her very cross face. There was no way I was doing anything that might make her shout at me in front of everyone.

At last Mrs Kingston showed signs of winding

up, and we were allowed to walk very slowly towards the back of the hall. There was a bit of pushing and shoving as everyone tried to find their name. Louise got there first and reported back.

'I'm with Kellie,' she said. 'Grace is on her own again, and Alice and Megan are together.'

I turned to Alice and we jumped up and down and hugged each other.

This was so great! Now I was going to be with Alice for English and Home Ec, and I had Kellie in all of my other classes.

This was going to be a totally fun term – I just knew it.

Chapter three

The first few weeks went by very quickly. Then one day, our new English teacher, Mr Dunne, came in to class rubbing his hands, and saying,

'Listen carefully, class, because I have some very big news.'

Alice nudged me.

'He's probably going to tell us that he got a new car, or something boring like that,' she said.

I giggled.

'No,' I whispered back. 'I bet he wants to tell us that he's discovered an exciting new book, all about full stops and commas and quotation marks.'

Alice giggled too, but stopped when she saw that Mr Dunne was staring at us.

'When Megan and Alice are ready,' he said, 'I'll tell you the news.'

We all sat up straight, and when the room was perfectly silent he continued.

'It's a competition,' he said.

Now everyone listened carefully. Competitions are usually a lot more fun than regular school work and they are much less likely to involve stupid grammar rules.

Mr Dunne continued.

'It's an essay competition.'

I started to smile. I *love* writing essays, and Mr Dunne nearly always gives me top marks when we have to do one. Maybe I could win. Maybe, for the first time since starting secondary school, I could stand out as someone special.

Sophie put her hand up.

'What kind of an essay do we have to write?'

she asked. 'Can we write about disco dancing?'

A few of the boys laughed, and everyone else groaned. Sophie is a disco-dancing champion, and she's also a champion at boring everyone to death by talking about disco dancing.

Mr Dunne sighed.

'No, Sophie,' he said. 'You can't write about disco dancing.'

Sophie put on a sulky face.

Then lots of hands went up together.

'What do we have to write about?'

'How much do we have to write?'

'Can we do it on the computer?

'What's the prize?'

Mr Dunne smiled.

'It's nice to see you're all so enthusiastic,' he said, ignoring Sophie who was muttering under her breath.

Then he continued.

'The essay has to be around three to four

hundred words long.'

There were a few groans from the kids who are always in trouble for not finishing their home-work.

Mr Dunne ignored them.

'You can do your first draft in your copies, but anyone who wants can type out their final draft on the computer. The topic of the essay is "The benefits of foreign travel".'

There were a few more groans from the back of the class.

Suddenly Sophie perked up.

'I went to a disco-dancing competition in England last year. Can I write about that?'

Mr Dunne sighed.

'Did you benefit from the trip?'

Sophie smiled happily.

'I got a silver medal. Look, I've got it here in my bag. Will I show you?'

I tried to hide my smile. Sophie had shown

everyone in the class that medal about five times already. It was probably almost worn out from all the times she had put it in and out of her school bag.

Before Mr Dunne could reply, a boy called Joe put up his hand.

'I've never been to a foreign country,' he said. 'So can I write about my holidays in Kilkee?'

Mr Dunne shook his head.

'Sorry, Joe, I don't think that would count,' he said. 'But don't worry. Anyone who has never been abroad can write about why they think a trip abroad would improve their lives.'

Joe put up his hand again.

'What if you don't think a trip abroad would improve your life?'

Mr Dunne shook his head crossly.

'Well you'll just have to pretend, won't you? But everyone has to write the essay, it will be good practice for you all. The first draft is your homework. I'll be collecting it on Monday.'

Now there were lots more groans.

Once again Mr Dunne ignored them. Maybe being half-deaf is a good thing in a teacher.

'The good news,' he said, 'is that there's a big prize. A very, very big prize. It's been donated by a past pupil of the school, and entry is limited to boys and girls who are currently in first year.'

Everyone sat up straight again and waited. Mr Dunne fumbled with a bundle of papers on his desk.

'Now where did I put that letter?' he muttered.

At last he waved a piece of paper in the air.

'Here it is,' he said.

The only sound was the slight rustle as Mr Dunne unfolded the letter and began to read silently.

Then he folded the letter and pushed it back into the envelope.

'Actually, I'm not supposed to tell you what the

prize is until tomorrow,' he said.

This time the groans were almost deafening.

'That's not fair,' said one of the boys from the back.

Mr Dunne gave a mean smile.

'Life's not fair,' he said, suddenly reminding me of something Marcus had said once.

Then we all had to open our workbooks and spend half an hour doing totally boring grammar.

*   *   *

Alice and I walked home with Grace, Louise and Kellie. Like us, the others had also been told about the competition, but not about the prize.

'I wonder what it is,' said Kellie.

'The teachers are making a big deal of it,' said Grace. 'So it must be totally great.'

'Maybe it's something stupid like a pencil case, and they're just getting us all worked up so we'll write good essays,' Alice said.

We all laughed and then Louise said.

'Very funny, Alice, but I bet you're wrong. We have to write about foreign travel, so I bet it's a trip abroad.'

Kellie sighed.

'I bet you're right. I'd so love to win a trip abroad. I'm going to start my essay tonight.'

'Me too,' said everyone except Alice.

'I'm not writing a single word until I know exactly what the prize is,' she said. 'Imagine all that wasted effort if the prize turns out to be something stupid.'

I didn't agree. I didn't care a whole lot what the prize was. I just wanted to win.

'I'm going to base my essay on my trip to France last summer,' I said.

Alice nudged me and giggled.

'What was the benefit of that?' she asked. 'A big soppy romance with a local boy?'

Sometimes I wished Alice didn't have such a long memory. I had to smile though. Alice had come to France the summer before, with my family and me, and we'd had a totally brilliant time, and I'd met a really nice boy called Bruno. Those sunny days seemed very long ago now.

We talked about the competition until we got home, and that night I wrote my essay. I went over and over it for ages until I was satisfied. Then I carefully put it into a folder and put it at the bottom of a drawer where it would be safe.

For once in my life I was going to do something great. I was going to write the very best essay and I was going to win the prize – whatever it was.

Chapter four

As soon as Mr Dunne came into class the next day, everyone rushed to ask him questions. In the end he held his hands up.

'OK, I surrender,' he said. 'I'll tell you what the prize is. But first you all have to sit down quietly.'

We all scuttled back to our desks and sat as quietly as we could while Mr Dunne rooted in his brief-case for the all-important letter. There was another long wait while he looked for his glasses, and by then we were all practically jumping

up and down in our desks, we were so excited.

Then he began to read. The letter was full of totally boring stuff at first, but finally Mr Dunne got to the good bit.

' … The student who writes the best essay will be declared the winner. The prize is …'

Here Mr Dunne stopped, just to tease us. Then he read on quickly.

' … The prize is four months at the world-famous École St Jean in Paris. In other words, the competition winner will go to school in France from the beginning of March until the end of June.'

Mr Dunne folded up the letter and put it back into the envelope. There was loads of excited chattering.

'Yuck,' said Sophie out loud. 'I'm not going to enter the stupid competition. I'd *hate* to go to school in France. You'd probably have to eat gross stuff like snails and frogs' legs and things.'

Joe laughed.

'See!' he said. 'I said yesterday that foreign travel wouldn't improve your life.'

Mr Dunne put on a very cross face.

'Now you're both just being very silly,' he said. 'The French are a very civilised people. I suspect they would have a more varied diet than that.'

Joe sulked – he doesn't take correction very well.

'I wouldn't want to go anyway,' he said. 'I like Kilkee. Who wants to go to stupid old France?'

Alice turned to me.

'Wow,' she said. 'Imagine school in France. How cool would that be?'

Jane put up her hand.

'We've only just started to learn French,' she said. 'How would we understand what's going on in the school?'

She was right. I could only say stupid stuff like 'I have a little sister' and 'Where is the nearest bank?'

'That's a good question, Jane,' said Mr Dunne. 'École St Jean is really an international school. There would be students there from all over the world, and teachers too. There would be a lot of French spoken, but you'd get plenty of help in the beginning. It really is a great opportunity for the winner.'

By now Alice was so excited she could hardly sit still in her seat.

'I am *so* entering that competition,' she said to me. 'Four months at school in France – that would be like something from an Enid Blyton book. You could make friends with girls from all over the world. It would be soooo exciting. I'm going to start my essay as soon as I get home.'

I didn't answer her. Instead I put up my hand.

'Yes, Megan,' said Mr Dunne.

'How many prizes are there?' I asked.

Mr Dunne had to take out the letter and read it again.

'Looks like it's just the one,' he said. 'Only one lucky winner gets to go to school in France.'

Everyone was still talking excitedly, but I did my best to tune out the noise.

I had to think.

Only one prize.

But if I won it, would I want it?

Would I really want to spend four whole months in France on my own?

Mostly I like being at home. I know Mum is a bit weird at times. (OK, so maybe I mean she's very weird most of the time.)

And Dad can be a bit annoying. (OK, so maybe I mean he can be very, very annoying when he tells stupid jokes in front of my friends and pretends to be all hurt when they don't laugh).

And Rosie can be a little bit of a pain when she comes into my room and messes up my stuff. (OK, so maybe I mean she drives me totally crazy when she messes up my stuff, and then thinks she can just get away with it because she's so small and so cute.)

But whatever. They're my family, and I love them, and I would hate to be away from them for too long.

And then there was Alice. Back when I was in sixth class, Alice spent a few months in Dublin with her mother and brother, and that was totally awful. How could I cope with four long months of us being apart?

Then I remembered Domino. What would I do if I had to go for four months without stroking her soft black fur?

How could I cope without feeling her sand-papery tongue licking my hand?

She'd practically be a grown-up cat by the time I got back …

I put up my hand again.

'Er ……Sir, if I ….. I mean …… a person

won the competition ... would the person *have* to take the prize?'

Mr Dunne scratched his head.

'That's a very strange question, Megan,' he said. 'I think the organisers might be a bit offended if the winner didn't accept the prize. But anyway, I can't see that happening. What kind of person wouldn't want to spend four months in a French boarding school?'

A person like me?

Jane put her hand up.

'What if you won the competition, and your parents didn't allow you to go to France?'

Suddenly I felt sorry for Jane. She's an only child, and her parents hardly let her walk to the local shop without them. There was no way they would allow her to go all the way to France on her own. I smiled at her to show that I knew how she felt.

'We've thought about that, Jane,' said Mr

Dunne. 'We've prepared a letter for you all to take home to your parents. It explains everything they need to know about the competition, and about the prize. At the end of the letter, there's a permission slip and a box for your parents to tick, letting us know if they would be willing to allow you travel to France. Everyone has to hand up a first draft, and a signed permission slip by Monday. Your essay will only be entered in to the competition if your parents are happy for you to accept the prize. Do you all understand?'

Everyone nodded, except for Joe, who was muttering, 'I understand that whatever happens, I'm not going to go to stupid, stupid France.'

Mr Dunne gave him an evil look.

'Oh, and by the way,' he said, 'you are *all* to bring back those signed permission slips, even if your parents don't want you to enter the competition. I want to know that you have all discussed it with your parents, and not made the decision on your own. You never know, Joe – maybe your parents would like the idea of four months without you!'

Joe stopped muttering and gave Mr Dunne an equally evil look.

Mr Dunne continued, 'Anyway, that's enough about that. Remember first drafts and signed slips in by Monday. Now take out your grammar books and open them at page twenty-two.'

So that was that.

I didn't want to win.

Now all I had to do was hope that Alice wouldn't win either, and then we could all live happily ever after.

Chapter five

Alice was a right pain as we walked home that afternoon. She kept going on and on about the competition. She didn't seem to notice that I wasn't as excited about it as she was.

'I am *so* going to win that competition,' she said. 'I know what I'm going to write about already. I thought about it all through history class. I've even got the first paragraph all planned in my head. Will I say it for you?'

I shook my head.

'It's OK, thanks.'

Alice looked kind of hurt, but she didn't say anything. After a while she spoke again. 'Have you decided what you're going to write about yet?'

I finished my essay last night. It's the best essay I've ever written and I think it might be good enough to win the prize.

I didn't say that though. I decided to avoid her question.

'I don't know why everyone's getting so excited,' I said. 'It's only a stupid old essay. Since when are essays such a big deal?'

Now Alice looked really shocked.

'But the competition—'

I interrupted her.

'I'm not even going to try. I don't *want* to win the stupid competition.'

Alice stopped walking. She stared at me like I

was a total idiot.

'But why not? That's crazy. You heard Mr Dunne describing the prize. Wouldn't you love four lovely long months in France? It would be like our summer holidays, only better.' She stopped and giggled. 'You might even meet Bruno again.'

Bruno had been really nice, and I wouldn't have minded meeting him again, but even the thought of that couldn't cheer me up. I just wished that Alice would stop talking about France.

Alice didn't notice that I wasn't enjoying our conversation.

'Or maybe you'd meet Pascal,' she said. 'Wouldn't that be a laugh?'

Pascal was Bruno's evil cousin, and I certainly would *not* want to meet him again. Last time I saw Pascal, Alice had dumped a bowl of lentil stew on his head. It was the funniest thing I had ever seen, but now, thinking about it, I didn't feel like laughing.

Alice just kept on talking.

'I bet they don't make you help in the kitchen in École St Jean,' she said. 'I bet you just sit down, and they wait on you, like you're a princess or something. Oh and I bet they have yummy buttery croissants for breakfast every morning. Think of it, Meg, four whole months without porridge. Wouldn't that be like all your dreams come true?'

I couldn't laugh at her joke. I couldn't even force myself to smile.

Didn't Alice get it?

Couldn't she see what was happening here?

I felt like crying while Alice kept on talking.

And then, all of a sudden, I didn't feel like crying any more, because suddenly I felt really, really cross.

'I don't get you, Alice O'Rourke,' I said. 'I

really don't. Remember all the crazy plans you made me help you with? Remember hiding under my bed? Remember that stupid thing with your mother's life coach? What was all that about? You spent half a year plotting and scheming to get back to Limerick, and now all you want to do is to leave again.'

Alice looked at me in surprise. She's not used to me getting cross like that – that's usually her job.

'But that was different,' she said.

'How was it different?' I asked.

Alice shrugged.

'Well, it just *was* different.'

I wasn't letting her away with stupid answers like that.

'Tell me how it was different,' I insisted.

Alice thought for ages.

'Well, that time, I didn't want to be away.'

'And this time you do?'

'Well, like I said, that time was different. I missed Dad, and—'

I felt like stamping my foot.

'But won't you miss your dad if you go to France? And your mum? And Jamie? And ...' I hesitated before saying the next words, and then I whispered them so softly I was afraid Alice wouldn't be able to hear them, '...... and won't you miss *me*?'

Alice turned and hugged me.

'Of *course* I'd miss you,' she said. 'I'd miss everyone, and especially you. I'd probably even miss Domino!'

I pulled away from her.

'Then why do it? Why enter the stupid competition?'

Alice took a step away from me, and looked at me like I was the crazy one.

'I'd miss you, but not so much that I'd turn down the chance to live in France for four months. I might never get that chance again. I have to go for it.'

She smiled at me, and that made me feel even worse.

Way back in primary school, Alice was the one who always came to my rescue when my old enemy Melissa bullied me.

When we started secondary school, Alice was the one who helped me to stand up to Marcus.

If Alice went away, who would stand up for me, and say smart things if I met more people like Melissa and Marcus?

What would I do without her?

I started to walk again, and Alice walked beside me, saying nothing.

Thoughts raced madly around, like they were fighting for space in my brain.

Was it that Alice didn't like me as much as I liked her?

Maybe she was fed up of me?

Was she tired of being my friend?

I could feel tears coming to my eyes.

What would Alice say if she saw me crying?

Would she laugh?

Would she think I was just a sad loser?

I quickly wiped my eyes with the back of my hand, and started to prepare a story about dust in my eyes.

And then Alice started to talk again.

'Even if I won, I'd only be away for four months. That's not so long. Maybe you could come and visit me for a long week-end or something. And you'd be OK here. You'd still have Grace and Louise and Kellie.'

Everything she said made perfect sense, but that didn't matter.

All I could think of was that Alice didn't care about going away from me.

'Anyway,' she said at last. 'It's stupid to fight about this. We're fighting over something that's probably never going to happen. There are almost a hundred kids in first year. Why would I be the one to win?'

I didn't answer.

There were two big problems with what she had said.

First, Alice is really, really good at writing essays.

And second, Alice is the most determined girl I know. Mostly she gets what she wants because she keeps on trying until things turn out the way she wants them. If Alice wanted to go to France for four months, I had a horrible feeling that was going to happen.

We were on our road by now.

'Want to come in for a while?' I said as we got to my house. 'Maybe Mum has made some organic flap-jacks.'

Alice shook her head. 'No thanks. I'd better go on home. I've got to … well, I've got to do my homework.'

I stood there and watched as she went up the drive of her own house. She opened the front door, then turned around and waved.

'See you later?' she called.

I knew exactly what she meant.

See you later, when I've finished writing the best essay in the history of the world.

Chapter six

Domino was sitting on her favourite plant in front of our door. When she saw me, she got up and stretched, arching her back like a cat in a cartoon. Then she came over and rubbed her soft fur along my legs. I bent down and stroked her and she gave a soft miaow.

Did she understand that I was upset?

Was she trying to make me feel better?

Or did she just want me to feed her?

Sometimes cats can be very hard to understand.

I let myself into the house, and found Mum

and Rosie in the kitchen. Rosie was chewing on a rice cake like it was the yummiest thing she had ever tasted.

'Want some, Megan?' she said, holding the soggy chewed side towards me.

I shook my head, hoping I'd never be hungry enough to want to eat something like that.

'Thanks, but no thanks,' I said.

'How was school?' asked Mum.

'Fine,' I said.

Mum *so* didn't need to hear the truth about my day. (And I *so* didn't need to hear her going on about how I should be more independent and not rely on Alice so much.)

'Would you like a glass of carrot and beetroot juice?' Mum asked. 'I've just made some.'

As she spoke she held up a glass full of frothy red stuff that looked like a science experiment gone very, very wrong.

I shook my head.

'No thanks. I've got loads of homework to do, so I'd better get started.'

I went into my room, sat down and opened my history book.

I looked at the same page for a very long time.

I couldn't think about history.

All I could think about was that Alice might be leaving again, and that this time it would be her own choice.

How could she do this to herself?

And how could she do it to *me*?

Alice wasn't my only friend anymore. Grace and Louise had been my friends for ages now. And Kellie, who I'd met during my first term in first year, was turning into a really good friend. She'd come to my house to see Domino lots of times, and she never once laughed at my crazy mum.

Grace, Louise and Kellie were lovely, but Alice was different. Alice was the one who made my life fun.

And I knew was that if she went away, nothing would be the same.

*   *   *

After a while, I closed my history book and pulled my essay from the drawer where I'd hidden it the day before. I read it again. It was really quite good – maybe even good enough to win the competition.

I couldn't take any chances. I took a deep breath and then I tore my precious essay up in to tiny little pieces, and threw them into the small waste-paper basket at my feet.

Then I quickly scribbled off three pages of stupid stuff about foreign travel. I made sure the page was really messy, and I made a few deliberate spelling mistakes. Then I shoved my copy in to my school bag, and lay on my bed to think about stuff.

I wasn't going to win the competition, and neither was Sophie, or Joe. I'd just better hope that, in some one of the first-year classes, there was a very clever boy or girl who loved writing essays, and who would *love* to go to France for four months.

And then Alice and I could stay together.

* * *

I stayed in my room for ages and ages.

A few times I took my phone out of my pocket. I kind of wanted to call Alice, but I couldn't do it. I *sooo* didn't want to hear her saying '*Sorry, Meg, I can't come out, I've got hours more work to do on this essay.*'

So I just lay there doing nothing

In the end, Mum came to look for me.

'Why are you just lying there?' she asked.

I shrugged.

'I just am,' I said. 'Is there a law against it?'

Mum made a face.

'Hmmm,' she said. 'If there isn't a law against it, there should be. I can see you're bored. Come into the kitchen, and I'll find a few jobs for you to do.'

I jumped up, and started to tidy my dressing-table.

'No,' I said quickly. 'I'm not bored. I'm not even the tiniest little bit bored. Look, I'm tidying my room.'

It was too late by then though. I should remember not to be cheeky to Mum, because she always gets me back in the end.

Mum folded her arms.

'You can do that later,' she said. 'Now come with me and you can help me to clean out a few of the kitchen cupboards. A bag of brown rice burst open this morning, and the grains have gone everywhere.'

I sighed and followed her.

Sometimes I really wished that just for one day, I could be the mother, and she could be the daughter.

Then she'd be sorry.

* * *

After tea, Alice called over.

'Did you get your essay finished?' she asked.

I nodded.

'What about you?'

She nodded too.

'Yes, but it's just the first draft. I want Mr Dunne to look at it, and tell me what he thinks. I'm going to do the final draft on the computer. I'm going to ask Dad to help me to lay it out properly, and I hope Mum can get me some fancy paper to print it on. She might even bind it for me.'

I didn't say anything. Alice stopped talking and looked at me carefully for a minute.

'I probably won't win, you know,' she said.

I still didn't say anything.

She just didn't get it.

Didn't she understand that in some ways it didn't matter whether she won or not?

Didn't she understand that half the problem was that she wanted to win in the first place?

Chapter seven

The next day was Saturday. I was still in my pyjamas when the door-bell rang.

'Get that, Megan, will you?' said Dad.

I slouched out towards the hall, hoping that it wasn't Alice. I didn't think I could bear to hear one more word about the stupid competition and the stupid, stupid École St Jean.

I opened the front door.

'Linda,' I gasped, as I saw who was standing there.

'Who were you expecting? The queen of Sheba?' laughed Linda as she hugged me.

'Sorry,' I said. 'I'm

really glad to see you.'

I was telling the truth. Linda is my mum's sister. Linda and Mum are very alike – except that Linda is younger and prettier and much more fun and doesn't believe in force-feeding poor innocent children with organic fruit and vegetables.

Linda followed me in to the kitchen, and there was more excitement as Mum and Dad and Rosie all got up and hugged her.

Mum made a big pot of herbal tea, and we all sat down at the kitchen table. Rosie climbed onto Linda's lap.

'Aaah,' said Mum. 'Isn't that sweet? She loves her Auntie Linda.'

'Chocolate,' whispered Rosie. 'Did you bring me some chocolate?'

I giggled. Mum would not be happy if she knew that Linda gives us chocolate every chance she gets.

Linda shrugged her shoulders, and did a very bad job of looking innocent.

Then she leaned in closer to Rosie.

'Later,' she whispered, and Rosie smiled so much it looked like her face was going to crack.

'It's lovely to see you and everything, Linda,' said Mum. 'But it's very early, and you didn't even tell us that you were coming.'

Linda didn't say anything. Her cheeks were turning a faint pink colour, and she kept patting her hair, like she was nervous.

I could see that there was something strange going on, but I couldn't figure out what it was.

Suddenly Rosie reached up and grabbed Linda's hand.

'That's a very pretty ring,' she said.

Mum nearly dropped her herbal tea.

'OMIGOD!' she shrieked. 'Linda. Your ring. That's a … you've got a … you're *engaged*?'

Linda was redder that ever, but she was nodding happily.

'Yes, Sheila,' she said. 'It's an engagement ring! I'm engaged! Isn't it great?'

Mum jumped up. 'But where's …?'

'Luka,' said Linda. 'His name is Luka.'

'Luka,' said Mum. 'Where's Luka?'

She opened the kitchen door and looked in to the hall, like she was expecting to find him sitting on the stairs.

Linda laughed.

'He's not with me. We only decided this yesterday. Luka flew back to Latvia to tell his family, and I got the first train here, so I could tell you all.'

There was another flurry of hugging and kissing. Rosie made us all laugh by jumping up and down and shouting 'happy, happy, happy' over and over again.

Then we all recovered and sat down to finish our herbal tea.

'So he's from Latvia?' said Mum.

Linda nodded happily.

'But he's been here for years. He speaks perfect English.'

Mum was shaking her head.

'I can't believe I'm going to have a brother-in-law. I can't believe I'm going to have a Latvian brother-in-law.'

'And I'm going to have a Latvian uncle,' I said.

'And at last I'll have someone to watch soccer matches with,' said Dad.

'Is Latvia near Dublin?' asked Rosie, making us all laugh some more.

'When is the big day?' asked Mum when we had recovered.

'We're not exactly sure yet. But we think in a few months time. We—'

Suddenly I jumped up.

'You're going to need a bridesmaid,' I said excitedly. 'I'd so much love to be your bridesmaid! My friend Louise was a bridesmaid last year, and she had such a fun time. She had this totally beautiful dress, and she looked like a princess. She might even lend it to me so you won't have to buy a new one. And Rosie could be your flower-girl. She'd be sooo sweet. She— '

Suddenly I noticed that everyone was staring at me. Linda looked embarrassed.

'I'm so sorry, Megan,' she said. 'It's not going to be that kind of wedding. We haven't decided on the details, but we know it's just going to be a simple affair. There won't be a bridesmaid or a flower-girl.'

Now I was embarrassed too. I felt sooo totally stupid. Rosie came over and hugged me.

'Don't be sad, Megan,' she said. 'When I'm big you can be my bridesmaid and you can wear Louise's pretty dress then.'

I hugged her back.

'Thanks, Rosie,' I said. 'And when I'm big, you

can be my bridesmaid – you and Alice.'

As I said the last words, I wondered if they were true.

Was Alice going to win the competition?

Was she going to go off to France and forget all about me?

When I got married, would Alice even be able to remember who I was?

Linda was holding out her hand and admiring her ring.

'Isn't this the most beautiful ring?' she said. 'I didn't want a ring at first, but Luka persuaded me.'

I wondered if I could track him down and get him to persuade her that she wanted a bridesmaid and a flower-girl too.

Linda took off the ring and handed it to Mum.

'Here, Sheila,' she said. 'Put it on and make a wish. Remember what Granny used to say? Anything you wish for on a new engagement ring has to come true.'

Mum put on the ring and closed her eyes. She was probably wishing for a vegetable sale in the local supermarket.

Then she handed the ring to me. I put the ring on, closed my eyes, and concentrated as hard as I could – and I wished that Alice wouldn't go to France.

Chapter eight

I was nearly ready for school on Monday morning when I remembered that I hadn't got my competition slip signed. Dad had already left for work, so my only option was to show it to Mum.

I waited until she was busy washing the porridge pot.

'Can you sign this please?' I said, as casually as I could, holding the slip and a pen towards her.

'What is it?' asked Mum without turning around.

'Oh, it's not important,' I said. 'It's just to say that I'm allowed to enter an essay competition. It's no big deal.'

I should have known better. Everything is a big deal to my mum.

She dried her hands and came to sit at the kitchen table.

'Let me see,' she said. 'What's the competition?'

I sighed.

'It's not important. All you've got to do is sign this paper, and then we can forget about it.'

Mum took the page from me and read it ever so slowly. Then she put it down and looked at me.

'Four months in France?' she said. 'The prize is four months in *France?*'

I nodded miserably.

'That's a very long time,' said Mum.

I nodded again.

Then Mum broke out into a conversation with herself.

'We'd miss you terribly.'

'But it would be a wonderful opportunity.'

'You'd be very lonely.'

'But it would be a chance to make lots of new friends.'

'The school might not have a healthy-eating policy.'

'I suppose we could go over and check it out.'

'I should talk this over with your father.'

'I know he'll agree that we should allow you to try for this.'

Then before I could do anything, she picked up the pen and ticked the 'yes' box, and then signed her name underneath.

I jumped up angrily.

I don't *want* to win,' I said. 'I don't want to go to France.'

'But—' began Mum.

'And I *won't* win,' I added.

'But how do you know that?'

Because I've deliberately written the worst essay in the world.

'I just won't.'

Mum narrowed her eyes.

'You know that when you do anything, it's important to do your best?' she said.

'I know,' I said, shoving the slip into my school-bag. 'And you're doing your best to make me late for school.'

Then I grabbed my lunch, and went out, slamming the door behind me.

* * *

A week later, Mr Dunne collected all the finished essays. He'd made me re-write mine, but I hadn't made it look any better. It was still untidy, and had lots of mistakes. When Mr Dunne read it, he'd soon see that it didn't even make a whole lot of sense. Now that Mum had signed the slip saying I could go to France if I won, I couldn't take any chances.

Mr Dunne looked at my essay as I handed it in.

'This is a bit careless, Megan,' he said. 'It isn't anything like your usual work.'

That's because this isn't any old work.

I could feel my face turning red.

'Sorry, Sir,' I said, but he had already moved on to take Alice's essay from her.

He looked at the beautiful binding, and then flipped through the perfect, neat pages.

'Well, Alice,' he said. 'This is more like it. Beautifully presented work. Well done.'

Alice smiled, and for a moment I felt like punching her, even though she hadn't done anything wrong.

* * *

The next week went by very, very slowly. I felt like I was walking around with a big black cloud hanging over my head. I felt that, at any moment, it was going to fall down on top of me, blocking out all the light.

One day, as we were walking home from school, Alice was driving me totally crazy.

'I could win the competition,' she said. 'I did my very best, and think I really could win.' Then she hesitated. 'But no,' she continued. 'I never win anything. I probably didn't win. But then maybe—'

'Enough already,' I snapped. 'You're so boring these days. Can't you talk about anything else except the stupid competition?'

Alice looked really hurt, and for a minute I was sorry for what I had said.

But then, when she started to talk about something else, I was glad.

If we ignored the competition, it just might go away.

Chapter nine

Then one afternoon, about a week and a half after we'd handed in our essays, all first-years were told to assemble in the hall for the last class of the day.

I stood next to Alice, with Kellie on my other side. Grace and Louise stood in front of us. We knew that the winner of the essay competition was going to be announced, and everyone was nervous. I felt cold and shivery and I had a horrible sick feeling in my stomach.

'I know I didn't win,' said Kellie. 'I tried my best, but I know my essay wasn't very good. I really only like writing stories about animals.'

'Better than stories about disco-dancing,' said Louise, and we all laughed nervous, forced laughs.

'I think Hannah in my class might win,' said Grace. 'I read her essay before she handed it up, and it's really good.'

Yessss! I felt like saying, but of course I couldn't.

Alice didn't say anything, which was *so* not like her.

Mrs Kingston went on for ages about boring stuff like tying our ties properly, and not running in corridors. We'd already heard the same speech about a hundred times, and I'd have fallen asleep if I hadn't been so nervous.

Next to me, Alice was all jittery. Her feet were jigging as if to some music that the rest of us couldn't hear, and when I looked at her, there was a funny sparkle in her eyes.

If she didn't win, I knew she'd be really disappointed.

But if she did win, I'd be devastated.

That probably means that I'm a very bad friend, but I can't help it.

Who ever said I had to be perfect?

*   *   *

At last Mrs Kingston mentioned the essay competition. She went on for ages and ages about the importance of learning how to write properly. She said that in a world of texts and e-mails good writing was getting harder to find. She said that even the people who didn't win had had a valuable exercise in writing. She said that the standard was particularly high. (Obviously she hadn't seen my essay.) Then, when I thought I was going to scream, she said the words I had been dreading.

'Now, it's the moment you've all been waiting

for. It's time for me to announce the winner.'

The sick feeling in my stomach got even worse.

'The standard was very high, or did I say that already?'

Yes, now just get on with it, and put me out of my misery.

Mrs Kingston continued, 'And since the standard was so very high, the school has decided to award a second prize of an MP3 player.'

I felt like kicking myself for writing such a bad essay. I'd *love* an MP3 player and there's zero chance of my mum or dad ever buying me one.

Mrs Kingston gave a small smile.

'And the second prize goes to … Hannah Lee!'

Hannah, who was standing near us, gave a small squeak of joy, and everyone around her began to pat her on the back and whisper to her until Mrs Kingston called for silence again.

Then she went on.

'And now for the first prize winner – the person who will be going to France for four months. I know you have already brought in signed permission slips, however as this is such an important prize, we took the precaution of telephoning the winner's parents this morning, just to make sure they'd allow their child to go abroad for a few months. And I'm happy to say that the winner's parents think it's a great idea for their daughter to—'

Mrs Kingston stopped suddenly, looking embarrassed.

At first I didn't understand.

'It's a girl,' whispered Kellie. 'A girl has won first prize.'

All around the hall, boys were muttering and looking disappointed, while the girls were even more excited than before.

In front of me Grace sighed.

'I know it's not me. My parents are in America,

and their mobiles aren't working out there.'

Louise put her arm around her. 'Don't worry,' she said. 'I know it's not going to be me either.'

Mrs Kingston was speaking again. 'And the winner is ....'

There was a silence that felt like it was a hundred years long, before Mrs Kingston finished her sentence.

' .... Alice O'Rourke!'

All around me everyone went crazy. Even people who hardly knew her, rushed over and hugged Alice. Everyone was clapping and cheering and stamping their feet. I gave Alice a small hug and then I was edged away by everyone else trying to join in with the excitement.

Suddenly Kellie was beside me.

'Isn't it so great?' she said.

I nodded, not daring to speak.

Kellie looked closer at me, and I hoped she couldn't see the beginnings of tears in my eyes.

'Hey, Megan,' she said. 'I'm sorry. Did you think you were going to win?'

I shook my head. 'No, I knew I was never going to win. I didn't even try.'

'But …'

Then she slapped herself on the forehead.

'I'm an idiot,' she said. 'You're going to miss Alice.'

Once again, I didn't dare to answer, afraid that, instead of words, sobs would come rushing out of my mouth.

Kellie put her arm around me.

'Don't worry,' she said. 'I know you'll miss her. We all will. But four months isn't really all that long. And in the meantime, you've got Grace and Louise and me. We'll look after you. You'll be fine – I promise.'

I nodded.

Kellie was being really nice, but it didn't make any difference. Without Alice, nothing was going to be the same.

I looked over to where Alice was surrounded by boys and girls, all pushing and laughing and trying to get close to her. She was like a film-star or something. Then she saw me, and she waved her arm, calling me over.

I started to move towards her, and then I knew I couldn't do it.

It was too hard.

I just *couldn't* pretend to be happy.

Then I realised that Kellie was still beside me.

'All I want is to go home,' I said, 'but what will Alice think?'

Kellie put her arm around me again.

'Just go,' she said. 'I'll think of an excuse to tell Alice. And maybe ... maybe I can tell her that you'll call for her later?'

I hesitated.

I didn't want to call for Alice later.

What was I supposed to say to her?

But I knew I had to brave.

'Sure,' I said, trying to smile. 'Tell her I'll call for her later.'

Then I slipped out of the hall by the side door, and walked slowly home on my own.

Chapter ten

When I got home, I let myself in through the back door. For once, Mum wasn't in the kitchen. I was glad, because I soooo didn't feel like one of her endless question sessions.

Maybe I could get to my room and pretend to be really busy with homework.

Maybe she'd leave me in peace for once.

I had safely tiptoed half way across the hall when Rosie appeared out of nowhere.

'Hi, Megan,' she said. 'You look very sad. Do you want me to play Snap with you?'

I shook my head, not trusting myself to answer.

'Monopoly?'

I shook my head again.

'Why are you sad?' she asked.

How could I explain?

'Did you fall down? Have you a pain in your tummy?'

Why couldn't it be as simple as that?

Then I spoke without really thinking.

'Rosie, who is your best friend at playschool?' She thought for a minute and then grinned.

'Charlie,' she said. 'He's funny. He— '

I interrupted her, 'What would you do if Charlie wanted to go away and leave you all on your own?'

Rosie didn't have to think very hard about this one.

'I would kick him very hard and make him cry,' she said. 'And then I would tell him not to go away from me.'

I had to smile.

What would Alice do if I went over to her place and started kicking her?

Would it make her change her mind about going to France?

Or would it make her call the police?

I leaned on the banisters and gave a big long sigh.

Why hadn't I paid more attention when Alice was plotting and scheming?

If she were in my place now, she'd know exactly what to do.

She'd have hundreds of mad ideas, and the only difficulty would be deciding which one to go for.

Alice is the one I always turn to for help, but what good was that to me now?

Hey, Alice I have a bit of a problem I need your help with. Only problem is – the problem is you.

How pathetic was that?

Suddenly Rosie put her arms around me. She's so small that she was sort of hugging my legs, with her face pressed up against the hard canvas of my school-bag.

'Don't be sad, Megan,' she said.

For one second I managed to hold it together – and then I lost it. Tears started to pour down my face, and I began to sob loudly.

Rosie pulled away from me in shock. She's not used to seeing me crying. She looked desperately up the stairs. I knew she was going to call Mum. I knew I had to stop her, but I was crying too much.

As I struggled to catch my breath, Rosie screamed at the top of her voice.

'Muuuuum! Megan is very sad. She's crying. I think you'd better come down here!'

I felt like punching Rosie, which was a bit mean, since she was only trying to be nice. She stood in the hall, waiting for Mum to come and make everything all right again.

I heard Mum's footsteps at the top of the stairs, and I raced into my room and threw myself on to my bed, ready for the inquisition.

Rosie ran in after me. She sat on the edge of my bed and held my hand.

'Rosie make you all better,' she said, not knowing that she was promising the impossible.

Seconds later, Mum was sitting on the bed too.

'What is it Megan?' she asked in a concerned voice. 'Are you sick? Has something happened at school?'

For a while I was too busy sobbing to answer. Mum sat there, rubbing my back, and waiting for me to finish.

After a while, it felt like I had cried every tear in my body. My throat hurt, and my eyes were all scratchy. I sat up and tried to stop the horrible sobbing noise that kept on escaping from my sore throat.

It was all too much for poor Rosie. She jumped off the bed.

'I'm going to play with my dollies,' she said, and she ran out of the room.

Mum was still stroking my back.

'Tell me, Megan,' she said. 'Just be brave and tell me. Nothing can be this bad.'

Easy for her to say.

She doesn't need friends.

All she cares about are carrots and broccoli and things that can't hurt you.

Mum was still waiting for me to answer.

And then, because I knew she'd wait for a hundred years if necessary, I told her why I was crying.

'It's Alice,' I said. 'She's won the essay competition. She's going to France. And she doesn't even care about leaving me. She's going to be gone for *four whole months*. I'm going to miss her so much. What am I going to do without Alice for four whole months?'

As I said the last few words, I started to cry again.

Then Mum was quiet for a long time – such a long time that I began to get seriously worried. Mum doesn't do quiet, it really isn't her style.

At last she spoke.

'Is that it, Megan?' she said. 'Have you told me everything?'

I nodded.

I felt a small bit better now that I'd told Mum exactly how I felt. In a funny way I was a bit like Rosie – part of me still believed that Mum could make everything all right again.

I wiped my eyes and wondered what Mum was going to do next.

Maybe she'd go and make me some hot chocolate and I could snuggle up in bed and enjoy its sweet, warm milkiness.

Maybe I could be snuggly and safe and cosy for a while.

Maybe I could forget all about Alice, and the competition, and the trip to France.

Just as I was imagining the sweet hot chocolate slipping down my sore throat, Mum stopped stroking my back. She sat up very straight.

'Megan, darling, don't you think that maybe you're being a small bit selfish?' she said.

This took me so much by surprise that I stopped sobbing at once.

Mum is supposed to be on my side.

She's *always* supposed to be on my side.

Even when I'm wrong she's supposed to be on my side.

It's her job.

So what on earth was going on here?

Mum didn't wait for my answer.

'Try and think of all the things that you have that Alice doesn't,' she said.

Well that wasn't too hard.

Alice hasn't got a crazy mum, who embarrasses

her at every opportunity.

Alice doesn't have to endure organic porridge every morning, followed by loads of super-healthy organic meals with brown things in them.

She doesn't have wardrobes full of lumpy knitted scarves and jumpers, and freaky home-made skirts.

But I knew what Mum meant.

Alice's parents don't live together any more.

Alice has to divide her time between her dad who lives next door to us, and her mum, who lives in an apartment up the road.

Things are a lot better now, but Alice has had a very tough time over the past year and a half.

How had I managed to forget that?

I could feel my cheeks becoming warm and pink. Mum was right. I was being selfish.

Mum smiled at me, to show me that she wasn't cross.

'I know you're sad,' she said. 'Your best friend is going away, so it's only to be expected. But think what a great opportunity this is for Alice. She deserves to have something nice happen to her. And four months seems like a long time now, but trust me, it will go quickly in the end. By this time next year, you'll wonder what all the fuss was about. So you have to be brave. Wish Alice well, spend time with your other friends, and wait for summer to come. Everything will be fine – I promise.'

I tried to smile, but I couldn't feel happy. I was too embarrassed for that.

Mum hugged me.

'It's OK, Megan,' she said. 'Everyone feels sorry for themselves every now and then. Sometimes it's OK to have a good cry.'

I hugged her back.

'Thanks, Mum,' I said.

Mum jumped up.

'Feeling better now?'

I nodded.

'Then I'd better go and see to the dinner. It's soya-bean bake – your favourite.'

I felt like crying again – whatever gave her the idea that I actually liked soya-bean bake?

How could *anyone* like soya-bean bake?

But now wasn't the time for arguing.

'Yummy,' I said, and I kept the smile on my face until Mum was gone and the door was closed firmly behind her.

And then I lay down and cried a few more tears.

Chapter eleven

I lay on my bed for a very long time.

I played with the small silver bus on a chain, that Alice had given me when I visited her in Dublin.

And after a while, I knew what I had to do.

Alice has always been my very best friend.

I was going to be happy for her, even if it killed me.

*   *   *

After ages, I got up and went in to the bathroom. I washed my face and brushed my hair.

'I'm calling over to Alice's place,' I called to Mum.

'OK,' Mum called back. 'But don't be late for tea. I don't know if I'll be able to keep Dad and Rosie away from your share of the soya-bean bake.'

I'd have laughed, but the sad thing is, I don't think she was joking.

*   *   *

I ran next door, glad that Alice was spending the night in her dad's house. If I'd had to walk all the way to her mum's place, I might have had time to change my mind.

I rang the doorbell, trying to ignore the part of me that hoped Alice wouldn't be there.

Alice answered the door. She was still fizzing with excitement as she led the way to her room.

'Isn't it the coolest thing ever?' she said. 'I wish you could have stayed at school a bit longer. Everyone was going crazy. Even some of the teachers hugged me. I know that's totally gross, but I didn't mind. Luckily Mrs Kingston didn't try to hug me, though. I had to go in to her office, and she told me all about the prize. And the best part was – she told me about the Easter holidays.'

Suddenly things didn't seem quite so bad. How could I have forgotten about Easter? It wasn't too far away.

'So you'll be coming home for Easter?' I said. 'That'll be sooo cool. We can do loads of great stuff together. You can tell me all about your school then. You can ......' I stopped talking as I noticed that Alice had a very strange look on her face. It was like a mixture of embarrassment and total happiness.

'I won't be home for Easter,' she said.

I didn't understand.

'You have to come home,' I protested. 'They can't keep you prisoner over there.'

She shook her head.

'I won't be a prisoner. The school organises a ski-trip during the holidays. I'll be going to the French Alps for ten days. Imagine! Ten whole days skiing.'

I couldn't imagine that. Maybe my imagination wasn't working very well that day, because all I could imagine was loads of boring days in Limerick without Alice.

Alice kept talking.

'Mrs Kingston gave me heaps of brochures and stuff for Mum and Dad to read and then I went back outside to the hall, and everyone was still going crazy and I wish you could have been there.'

'I........,' I began, but Alice interrupted me.

'Kellie said you had to do jobs for your mother. I hope it wasn't too boring.'

It was nice of Kellie to help me, but I knew it was time to tell the truth.

'Kellie was just trying to protect me,' I began.

Alice giggled.

'Protect you?' she asked. 'From who? From Mrs Kingston and the crazy hugging teachers?'

I shook my head.

'No,' I said slowly.

This was really too hard, but I knew I had to continue.

'Kellie was kind of protecting me from myself. You see ...... I didn't want you to win that prize,' I said.

Alice looked puzzled.

'I know you sort of said that before,' she said.

'But I didn't think you really meant it.'

I nodded sadly.

'I did. I was sorry when Mrs Kingston said that you'd won. I wasn't happy for you – not even for one second. That's why I had to go away. I couldn't bring myself to congratulate you.' I put my head down. 'I'm sorry,' I whispered.

Alice didn't answer. She sat down on her bed and stared at me. Now she looked even more puzzled than before, and all of a sudden, I could see why.

Alice is so kind and generous, she would never think of being upset if I won. If my essay had been the best, Alice would have been the first to hug and kiss me. By now she'd be lending me loads of her cool clothes, and helping me to pack my bags and book my flights.

I was lucky to have a friend like her.

I gave her a huge smile that wasn't even pretend.

'Congratulations,' I said. 'I hope you have a really, really fantastic time in France.'

Alice jumped up and hugged me.

'Thanks, Meg,' she said. 'You're the best.'

Chapter twelve

There were only two weeks left before Alice was due to go to France, and I made up my mind that I was going to make the most of them. There would be plenty of time for being sad when she was gone.

Grace, Alice and I were in a Home Ec group together. Usually we took turns to cook, but since Alice was going away, Grace and I decided to let her cook for her last two weeks.

'That's really nice

of you,' said Alice when we told her.

Grace and I just smiled. Alice still didn't know how much we loved the days when she cooked. Home Ec was never boring when Alice was anywhere close to the cooker.

On the next cookery day, Alice brought the ingredients for Madeira cakes. Our teacher, Miss Leonard seemed to be in a very good mood when we got into class, and we soon discovered why.

'Alice,' she said with a huge smile. 'I hear that you're going to be leaving us soon.'

Alice smiled back.

'I know,' she said. 'Sorry about that. I know you're going to miss me. But don't worry, I'll be doing Home Ec in France too, so I'll be able to practise everything I learned here. I'll tell everyone about you, though. I'll tell them you taught me everything I know.'

Miss Leonard's smile faded. She looked like someone who had a very sour lemon stuck between her lips and her teeth.

Alice is a total disaster in the kitchen, and I figured that Miss Leonard would not want anyone to blame her for that.

'Well, whatever you think best, Alice dear,' she said. 'Now switch on your oven and then you can start to set out your ingredients.'

For once, Alice had brought the right ingredients and, with help from Grace and me, she managed to mix up the cake without any major incident. (As long as you don't count the big lump of Madeira mixture that somehow took off and got stuck to the ceiling.)

The fun started when Alice went to put the cake into the oven.

'Whoops,' she said. 'I forgot to switch the oven on. I wonder if that matters?'

I shook my head.

'You idiot.' I said. 'Of course it matters. The cake will never be ready by home time. I think you should tell Miss Leonard.'

Alice shook her head.

'No way,' she said. 'I don't want her losing her good opinion of me. I'll just turn the oven up to the highest it can go, so the cake will cook faster.'

As she spoke she turned the oven on, shoved the cake inside, and slammed the door.

Grace made a face. 'I don't think that's a good idea, Alice,' she said.

I *knew* it wasn't a good idea, but before I could say anything, Miss Leonard was clapping her hands.

'Stop talking, Grace and Alice,' she said. 'Come over here to this table, so I can show you all how to make butter icing.'

Everyone went over to a corner of the room, where Alice did her best to drive Miss Leonard crazy by asking stupid questions about butter icing.

After a while, Jane, who's usually very quiet,

put up her hand.

'What is it Jane?' asked Miss Leonard.

Jane went red.

'Er … I could be wrong, … but I think I smell something burning,' she said. 'And I think it might be coming from over there.'

She pointed across the room, and at once everyone turned around to see wisps of dark smoke oozing from the door of one of the ovens.

'Alice,' muttered Miss Leonard. 'What have you done this time?'

'How does she know it's me?' asked Alice.

Grace and I grinned.

'Lucky guess, I suppose,' I said, and even Alice had to laugh.

We laughed a bit less as Miss Leonard ran over, opened the oven door, and had to step backwards as a huge cloud of thick, black smoke poured out of the oven.

Then everyone stopped laughing altogether as there was a sudden piercing shriek.

Alice went pale.

'Is that …… the fire alarm?'

I nodded.

'Sounds like it to me.'

'Omigod, there must be a fire somewhere,' screeched Laura, who's not very quick about copping on to things.

Miss Leonard grabbed some oven gloves, pulled Alice's smoking cake from the oven, and dropped it into a sink full of water.

She switched off the oven, then she turned and glared at Alice.

'There's no danger, any more,' she said. 'So there's no need to panic. But we have to obey the fire rules. Outside everyone, nice and calmly, and go to your designated assembly spots in the school-yard.'

We all did as we were told and filed outside.

I felt like laughing, but I didn't dare. Alice was standing next to me, and Miss Leonard looked like she would happily have killed her.

Seconds later, six hundred pupils and a large number of cross-looking teachers were lined up in the school-yard.

Miss Leonard walked along our line, counting us to make sure that everyone was where they were supposed to be.

'Er, Miss?' said Alice, as she went by. 'Do you think my cake will be OK if I put extra butter icing on it?'

Miss Leonard stopped walking and stared at Alice. Her face went pale – probably from the effort of not screaming.

'That's a "no" then,' said Alice. 'Still, there's always next week. What are we making next week? I hope it's something hard – I feel like a challenge.'

At last Miss Leonard found her voice.

'I don't know about everyone else,' she said. 'But next week *you*, Alice, are making salad.'

Then she marched off to try to explain everything to Mrs Kingston.

Alice turned to Grace and me.

'It's a terrible pity that happened,' she said. 'I've a feeling that Miss Leonard was just getting to like me. What do you think?'

But Grace and I couldn't answer.

We were too busy laughing.

Chapter thirteen

Much too soon it was almost time for Alice to leave.

She was all excited when she called for me before school on the Monday of her last week – so excited that she didn't even scream when Domino rubbed up against her leg.

'My plane tickets arrived this morning,' she said. 'And all the details of how I'm going to get to École St Jean. At last it feels real.'

It had felt real to me for ages, but I didn't say this.

'It's going to be so, so cool,' said Alice. 'I just can't wait to get there.'

I tried very hard, but I couldn't think of

anything to say to this.

I was still dreading Alice leaving, but in a funny way, I kind of hoped that she'd just hurry up and go.

I hoped that we could soon get all the sad good-byes over with, and then I could start to look forward to her coming back again.

And very deep down, I couldn't help hoping that something would happen to stop her going at all.

I couldn't help thinking about the wish I had made on Linda's engagement ring.

Could it really come true?

I didn't want anything really bad to happen, of course. I wasn't thinking of a bomb, or an earthquake or anything like that. I was just thinking of something a bit bad, like a teachers' strike or an epidemic of food poisoning at the French school, so it would have to be closed down – for about four months.

That wasn't such a bad thing to wish for.

Or was it?

And what did it matter anyway?

How could an engagement ring be that powerful?

How could a thin band of gold and diamonds change anything?

But maybe ......

'Hello? Earth calling Megan. Are you in there?'

I suddenly realised that I was leaning on the front door frame, with a stupid sad look on my face.

'Sorry, Alice,' I said. 'I was just trying to remember if I put my maths homework into my school-bag.'

'Whatever,' said Alice. 'Now we need to hurry or we'll be late.'

I bent down to give Domino her morning cuddle, and then Alice and I set off for school.

*   *   *

That afternoon, Alice and I walked home together as usual.

'Want to come in to my place for a while?' I asked as we got to my gate.

'I'd love to,' she said. 'But I've got to go home. I've got to sew name-tags on to all my clothes. Even my knickers.'

I giggled.

'Sounds like fun.'

Alice made a face. 'Not. But you can come and help ... er, I mean, watch me if you like.'

I hesitated.

'I should go home first,' I said.

Alice pulled my arm.

'Don't go home. You know your Mum will have hundreds of boring jobs for you to do. And ...'

'And what?' I said when she stopped in the

middle of the sentence.

She went red.

'And I was supposed to sew on the name tags last night, but I got bored after twenty minutes. And Dad said if they're not done when he gets home from work, he's going to take my phone.'

I laughed.

'OK, but I can't stay long or Mum will be worried.'

We went into the house and up to Alice's bedroom. There I quickly discovered that Alice is as bad at sewing as she is at cooking. She had only managed to sew one name-tag on to a t-shirt, and it looked like a stray gust of wind would be able to rip it off in seconds.

She happily handed me the needle and thread, and she chatted to me while I sewed on what felt like hundreds of name-tags on to every item of clothes she owned.

'What would I do without you?' she asked, as I

cut off the final thread.

You'll find out in a few days.

I didn't say this though.

I jumped up. 'Gotta go, or Mum will have a search party out looking for me.'

Then I picked up my schoolbag and went home.

Chapter fourteen

'Domino,' I called as I walked up the drive way. 'I'm home. It's time for your dinner.'

To my surprise, Domino wasn't curled up in her usual place on the flower-pot on the front step.

'Domino,' I called. 'Where are you, you bold kitty?'

There was no miaow, and no welcoming

rubbing of her soft fur against my legs.

'Mum, have you seen Domino?' I asked when I went inside.

Mum shook her head.

'Not since this morning. She was outside when I was hanging out the washing. She's probably gone off exploring. I wouldn't worry about her.'

Despite Mum's words, I couldn't help worrying. I think Domino must have had a scary experience before she strayed in to our garden last year. She's a very timid little creature, and she never really goes anywhere. She just hangs around our house and garden where she knows she'll be safe.

'I'll help you look for Domino,' said Rosie.

She followed me outside and helped me to search the garden and the garage and the lane at the back of the house. After twenty minutes of searching all we found was an old doll of Rosie's that had been missing for months.

'Any luck?' asked Mum as we went back inside.

I shook my head.

Mum came over and hugged me.

'Poor Megan. Now you know what it's like to be a mum,' she said. 'All mums worry too much. It's our job. But I'm sure Domino is fine. She'll get hungry, and she'll be back before long.'

All through tea-time, I listened for Domino's miaow from outside, but all I could hear was the traffic at the end of our road. The only good thing was, I was so worried about Domino that I barely tasted the mashed parsnips that Mum piled up on my plate.

After tea, I called for Alice, and told her about Domino.

She hugged me.

'You poor thing,' she said. 'I'll help you to look for her.'

So the two of us went up and down our road,

and all the roads nearby, rattling Domino's food box, and calling her name.

We got lots of funny looks from passers-by, but even though we searched until it was dark, we still couldn't find her.

I felt like crying when I got home. I didn't want to go to bed, but Mum insisted.

'I'm sure Domino's just gone on a little adventure. Dad and I will look outside before we go to bed,' she said. 'And if we find her, we'll bring her in to you, OK?'

I nodded, knowing that there was no point in arguing with Mum.

Even though it was cold, I left my bedroom window open. Domino knew which room was mine and, if she came back, maybe she'd sneak inside.

I woke up lots of times in the night, hoping that I'd feel Domino snuggled up next to me. But there was no soft fur, no sandpapery tongue on my arm, no warm, curled-up bundle.

No Domino.

*　　*　　*

In the morning, before I even got dressed, I raced out to the garden calling Domino's name. The damp grass was cold on my bare feet, but not as cold as the feeling in my stomach. Domino had never been away for long before. She'd never wandered off for more than a few minutes. She was much too small to spend a whole night out on her own.

I called and called, but there was no answering miaow. All I could hear was the wind in the trees, and the chirping of birds.

Why were they so happy?

Didn't they know my baby was lost?

When I got back inside, Mum made me eat a bowl of porridge, but it almost choked me.

'Can I stay home from school?' I asked. 'Please, Mum. Just this once. I need to look for Domino.'

Mum shook her head.

'Sorry, love. I know you're worried, but you have to go to school. As soon as I've cleared up the breakfast things, Rosie and I will go out and look for Domino. We'll have lots of time before she goes to playschool. How does that sound?'

I didn't answer. The only sound I wanted to hear right then was the sound of Domino purring, or the slurpy sound she makes when she laps milk from her saucer.

I went and got dressed, and was just ready when Alice called for me.

'Did Domino come home?' she asked as we walked out the gate.

I shook my head, trying not to cry.

Alice put her arm around me.

'We can look for her now – on our way to school,' she said. 'You never know. She might be around the next corner.'

We came to lots of corners, but Domino wasn't

around any of them.

All the way to school, we called Domino's name. We almost made ourselves late by looking under every parked car, and inside every bush and hedge. As we walked, I hardly dared to look at the road, afraid that I'd see a small crushed body lying there.

By the time we got to school, we had seen five cats, but none of them was as sweet and precious as my little Domino.

I was glad we had English first, so that Alice could stay with me. She sat beside me, and smiled sympathetically any time I looked at her.

It didn't help though.

Nothing could help.

Mr Dunne was rattling on about sentence structure, but I couldn't concentrate on what he was saying.

All I could think of was Domino.

Was she hurt?

Was she frightened?

Was she cold?

Was she hungry?

Was she wondering why I wasn't there to save her, like I did way back when I first found her in my back garden?

Suddenly I realised that Mr Dunne had asked me a question. Alice saved me by whispering the answer, which I repeated like a parrot.

Mr Dunne gave me a funny look, but didn't say anything.

I felt like putting my head down on my desk and crying buckets of hot tears.

In a few days, Alice would be gone, and now Domino was missing too.

What was I going to do?

Chapter fifteen

That afternoon, I ran the last few hundred metres home from school, hoping to find Domino back in her usual place on the flowerpot.

She wasn't there though. All I could see was the flattened earth, and the squashed plant that Mum had stopped giving out about months ago.

I opened the front door and stepped in to the hall.

'Megan,' called Mum. 'I have a great surprise.'

'Domino,' I called and raced in to the kitchen.

My face fell when I saw Linda sitting at the kitchen table.

'Oh,' I said. 'It's you.'

Linda got up and hugged me. 'Well that's a lovely welcome for your favourite aunt,' she said.

I went red.

'Sorry,' I said. 'It's really lovely to see you. It's just that my cat, Domino …'

Linda smiled sympathetically.

'I know,' she said. 'Sheila told me all about Domino, and I'm really sorry. Luka's outside in the garden looking for her.'

It took a moment for her words to sink in properly.

'Luka?' I said in the end. 'He's here?'

Linda laughed.

'Yes, he's here. I thought it was time for him to meet my family.'

Just then the back door opened and a man walked in. He was tall, and friendly-looking.

'You must be Megan,' he said, coming over to shake my hand. 'I've heard a lot about you.'

I could feel my face going hot and red.

I hoped that Luka hadn't heard how Alice and I had once tried to make Alice's dad, Peter, fall in love with Linda to make Alice's mum jealous.

'Er … I haven't heard a whole lot about you ……. yet,' I said, which made everyone else laugh, and made me feel like a total idiot.

Suddenly I forgot my embarrassment. I wondered if Linda had changed her mind about having bridesmaids.

'Is the wedding all arranged?' I asked. 'Have you decided on the details?'

Linda smiled.

'Not exactly. But I'm afraid we're still not

going to have bridesmaids.'

I put my head down. I was used to Mum reading my mind – I didn't know that Linda could do it too.

I wondered if it ran in the family.

I wondered if I'd be able to read my children's minds.

I wondered if I'd want to.

'You must have some plans made,' said Mum. 'Have you got a wedding dress? The one I wore is still in the attic. Don't you remember it, Linda? I borrowed it from Granny's friend, Eleanor, but she died before I got a chance to give it back.'

I giggled.

'Mum, I don't think Linda would want some dead old lady's dress. She's going to a wedding, not a fancy dress party. She wants to look nice.'

Linda gave me a grateful look, which almost made up for the hurt one that Mum gave me.

'Thanks, Sheila,' said Linda. 'But I'm going to

buy a new dress. Luka wants me to get a blue one. He says blue brings out the colour of my eyes.'

She gazed lovingly at Luka, and he gazed just as lovingly back at her.

I couldn't make up my mind if it was totally romantic, or grossly sick and soppy.

Mum still looked offended, and guilt made me speak again.

'Mum got a gorgeous dress for my Confirmation. She got it in O'Donnell's in town. There's a really nice lady in there who helped her to pick it out. Maybe you could go there and she could help you to choose something.'

Mum smiled at me, which made me feel even worse.

'That's a good idea,' said Linda. 'I've always liked that shop. Maybe I'll come down again in a few weeks time, and we can all go and pick something out together.'

'And what about a wedding meal?' asked

Mum. 'Have you anything planned?'

Linda shook her head.

'No. We're having a simple ceremony in a registry office, and then we'll just go home. We might invite a few friends back to our new flat for coffee.'

Suddenly Mum slapped the table.

'Well *that* certainly isn't going to happen.'

Everyone looked at Mum in surprise, especially Luka who must have been wondering if he was marrying into a crazy family.

'Er … Mum …' I began, but she interrupted me.

'No sister of mine is "just going home for coffee" after her wedding. After all, what would Luka's family think of us?'

'I think they will think you are very nice people,' said Luka politely, but Mum ignored him.

'You can have the ceremony in the registry office here in Limerick. And then you're coming here – you and anyone else you want to invite, and we'll celebrate properly. I'll cook a lovely meal for everyone.'

Linda and I looked at each other. Mum's idea of a lovely meal, isn't exactly the same as what most people in the world think of as a lovely meal. Mum's perfect meal would definitely involve lots of beans and brown rice and organic vegetables.

But before Linda could say anything, Luka had decided for her.

'Oh, Sheila,' he said. 'That's the nicest thing anyone has ever offered us. We'd love to accept, wouldn't we Linda?'

And then I understood that love can do very strange things to people's brains because Linda just smiled happily at Luka, and nodded.

'Sure, we would. Thanks, Sheila.'

And Mum looked like she'd just won the lottery.

And suddenly I realised that ten whole minutes had passed without me thinking of Domino at all. And then I felt sadder than ever.

Chapter sixteen

Linda and Luka left shortly after that. Linda wanted to introduce Luka to her best friend from school, and then they were going back to Dublin.

Mum offered to cook dinner for them before they left, but Linda said no.

I suppose she wanted Mum's cooking to come as a surprise to Luka.

After a while the door-bell rang again.

'That must be Linda back again,' Mum said. 'I bet she's decided to stay for dinner after all. I knew she wouldn't be able to resist. I'd better put on some extra lentils.'

But when I opened the front door I saw Alice, with Grace, Louise and Kellie.

'We're the official search party,' said Alice. 'We've come to help you to look for Domino.'

'I've made some "Lost" posters to put up,' said Kellie. 'I made them on the computer, and I put on the photo of Domino that you gave me.'

'And I've brought staplers so we can attach them to telephone poles,' said Louise.

'Well aren't you a lucky girl to have such nice friends,' said Mum. 'Now off you go, and, Megan, be back in time for dinner.'

We divided up the posters, and then Kellie, Alice and I went one way, leaving Grace and Louise to go the other way. We searched for ages, stopping every now and then to staple a poster on to a telegraph pole.

Alice stopped every single person we met, and

asked if they'd seen Domino.

Some people walked away quickly, as if they thought she was crazy.

Some people were really nice, and seemed sorry that they couldn't help us.

But no one at all could remember seeing a little black cat with a tip of white on her tail, and a small red collar around her neck.

In the end my legs were tired and my throat was sore from calling Domino's name. We went back towards home and we met Grace and Louise outside Alice's house. Grace shook her head when she saw us.

'Sorry, Megan,' she said. 'We've had no luck. But we've put up heaps of posters.'

'Maybe someone is minding Domino,' said Louise. 'And they'll bring her back to you once they find out where she lives.'

I knew Louise was trying to be nice, but I couldn't believe what she said. Domino loves me, and I knew that if she could, she'd come right back home to me – home to where she belongs.

It was going to be dark soon, and it was time for everyone to go home. We all hugged, and I went back inside.

Mum was extra nice, and after dinner she even let me watch TV for half an hour, but it didn't help.

*   *   *

That night and the next day passed in kind of a blur. News travelled quickly, and everyone seemed to know about Domino. Wherever I went, everyone was really nice to me. I was grateful, but it didn't make me feel any better.

Then it was Thursday, and the third night that Domino had been missing. At nine o'clock, I checked the garden one more time, and then I went to my bedroom. It was early, but I needed to be on my own for a while.

All I could think about was Domino.

My poor little kitten.

She was so small, and so defenceless.

How could she survive for so long without me to feed and mind her?

Would I ever again see her cute green eyes?

Would I ever again stroke her soft black fur?

And, as if losing Domino wasn't bad enough, in two more days, Alice would be leaving for France.

I'd have to be brave. I'd have to pretend to be happy for her. I'd have to act like everything would be just fine without her.

And how was I going to manage that?

Maybe Alice would change her mind.

Maybe she'd decide she wasn't brave enough to go to France all on her own.

Maybe something would happen so that she couldn't go.

Maybe I'd get up in the morning to find that

this was all a bad dream.

I put out the light and lay down. Then I closed my eyes and waited for sleep to rescue me.

*   *   *

I woke up while it was still dark.

I sat up in bed and rubbed my eyes.

Had I heard something, or was it the remnant of a dream?

And then I heard it again.

It definitely wasn't a dream.

I knew that sound.

It was a miaow.

It was a kitten.

And I knew for sure it was *my* kitten!

I jumped out of bed, raced over to the window and opened it.

And there on the windowsill was my … filthy … dirty … battered and tattered ... exhausted-looking Domino.

She gave a small, weak miaow, and then sort of collapsed into my arms.

I brought her inside, closed the window and switched on the light.

The poor kitty looked like she'd had a terrible time. She felt so light and thin in my arms that she was like a cat from a dream. But she was real, and she was alive, and she was licking my hand with her rough sandpapery tongue. Her fur wasn't soft and smooth like it was supposed to be, but I didn't care. I held her up to my face, and wet her dirty fur with my happy, happy tears.

Still holding Domino, I tip-toed into the kitchen, and poured some milk into a saucer.

Domino lapped it and then kept lapping, almost like she wanted to lick the painted flowers right off the saucer.

I quickly got her some of her food, which she gobbled up in seconds.

I found an old cloth under the kitchen sink,

and used it to wipe of the worst of the dirt from her fur. She had a small cut on one of her paws, but it didn't look too serious, and Domino didn't mind me wiping it clean.

Then we went back into my room, and I climbed into bed, with Domino cuddled up next to me.

'Where were you?' I asked. 'What happened to you? Why didn't you come back sooner?'

Of course she didn't answer, and soon I was too tired to ask any more.

I closed my eyes and slept soundly.

Chapter seventeen

I woke up to find Mum shaking me.

'I see your baby's back,' she said.

I knew she was glad, because there was a big mucky stain on my bed where Domino was lying, and Mum wasn't even cross.

I sat up, and cuddled Domino, happier than ever to see her.

Mum laughed.

'I'm very pleased for you, Megan,' she said. 'I'm glad that Domino's back, and not looking in too bad shape. Now get up or you'll be late for school, and you don't want that. It's Alice's last day, remember?'

Suddenly I remembered all too well. Domino might be back, but still everything wasn't perfect.

After breakfast Domino was back on her usual place on the plant pot outside the front door. It was almost like she'd never been away.

I stroked her even more than usual while I waited for Alice to arrive.

'No more mad adventures,' I said. 'I don't know where you've been, but I don't want you going there again. You stay right here, and I'll be back at half-past three.'

Domino just stretched and yawned, and made herself more comfortable in the sunshine.

Ten minutes later, there was no sign of Alice.

I went next door to call for her, wondering how she could possibly have overslept on her last day.

I rang the bell, but there was no answer. I rang

again, but still no one appeared.

I stood on Alice's front doorstep wondering what could be going on. Every morning she calls for me, and she's never late.

I tried ringing her mobile, but as usual, it was switched off.

Mum appeared at our front door.

'Why aren't you on your way to school?' she asked.

I explained.

'Could Alice have stayed at her mum's place last night? She might have changed her plans because of it being her last day,' suggested Mum.

I grinned. That had to be it.

'Thanks, Mum,' I said, as I headed off for Alice's mum's apartment.

When I got there, I rang the buzzer, but once again there was no answer.

I rang again.

Still no answer.

I began to feel a bit cross.

Why would Alice go to school without me?

She *never* goes to school without me.

We're *supposed* to go to school together.

It's what we do.

I walked towards school, meeting Grace and Louise on the way.

'Where's Alice,' asked Grace.

I shrugged, and tried not to sound hurt.

'I'd love to know. She must have gone to school early or something.'

We walked the rest of the way to school, and when we got there I immediately began to look for Alice. I checked the cloakroom, the toilets, her classroom, and the corridor where her locker is. There was no sign of her, and no one had seen her.

I met Kellie, and told her the story.

'Maybe she had to go to France early,' she suggested.

'She wouldn't,' I said. 'I know she wouldn't go without saying good-bye to me.'

Suddenly I realised that maybe she would.

Maybe she was afraid to say good-bye to me.

Maybe she was afraid that I'd make a big scene and embarrass her.

After all, I'd made a huge fuss about the trip to France before Alice had won the competition, before she'd even finished writing her essay.

Maybe she was already half-way to France.

And how could I blame her for not trusting me to be mature about it all?

*   *   *

Alice didn't show up at school at all, and the day dragged on and on. Every class seemed to last for hours.

Last class was Home Ec. After the fire-alarm drama the week before, Miss Leonard wasn't taking any chances, and she had decided that we were all making salad. Alice was supposed to be bringing in the ingredients for our group, but of course she wasn't there. Grace and I had to join other groups, and it was totally boring.

Still, I figured I might as well get used to it.

Nothing was fun without Alice.

*   *   *

When I got home, I was happy to see that Domino was exactly where I had left her on the flower-pot on the front doorstep.

I wasn't happy to see Mum standing at the front door, waiting for me.

She was pale, and her hair was even messier than usual.

'Megan,' she said. 'Something terrible has happened.

Chapter eighteen

Mum brought me inside and sat me down at the kitchen table. She put a glass of milk in front of me, but I couldn't bring myself to even pick it up. There was no way I was going to drink it.

'What's wrong?' I asked. I knew something scary was going on.

'It's Alice,' said Mum, and then she stopped talking and put her hands over her face. Suddenly I felt very afraid.

'What is it?' I asked. 'Just get on with it and tell me.'

When Mum spoke, her voice was weak and shaky.

'Last night, just before bed-time, Alice suddenly told Peter that she wanted to go out. She said she'd only be gone for a few minutes. Peter wasn't worried. He thought maybe she was going to come here or go to her mum's place. But half an hour later she still wasn't back. Then Peter got worried. He was just on his way to see if she was here when he heard the sound of an ambulance, far away, right at the end of Shelbourne Road. And that gave him a very bad feeling, so he ran down there, and ...'

Mum stopped talking again.

I wanted to shake her, to make her tell the story quicker, and yet I didn't want her to get to the end.

I was afraid of the end of the story.

Mum looked up and started to speak again.

'When Peter got there, they were just putting

Alice into the ambulance.'

'And is she …?'

'She's alive. She's in hospital,' said Mum. 'She's unconscious, and she's got a badly injured leg, but she's alive.'

I hardly dared to ask the next words.

'And is she going to be OK?'

Mum tried to smile, but didn't do a great job.

'They hope so.'

'What happened to her?' I asked. 'Was she hit by a car?'

Mum shook her head.

'That's the strangest thing. No one can figure out what happened. They don't know what Alice was doing, or why she was there. She was on the footpath outside the old empty house at the end of Shelbourne Road. A man living nearby heard a scream, and he went out and found her lying on the ground. She was unconscious, so he called an ambulance, and ……… well that's it.'

'Can I go and see her.'

Mum shook her head again.

'I'm sorry, Megan. Peter was here a while ago. He had to come home from the hospital to pick up a few things, so he came in to let us know what had happened. He said she's too sick for visitors. Only her family is allowed near her. In case … well in case she wakes up.'

Suddenly I thought of something else. 'What about France? Will she be able to go to France?'

Mum shook her head.

'I'm afraid France is out of the question now.'

I put my head down.

It was all my fault.

I'd been wishing and hoping that something would happen so that Alice couldn't go to France, and now my wish had come true.

And my best friend was unconscious in hospital.

I wondered if I could unwish my wish.

Or could I get Linda's ring and make a new wish?

Could I wish that Alice was right next to me, laughing her loud laugh, and making me feel happy just by being there?

Suddenly mum was hugging me.

She was crying, but I managed to hold back my tears. Tears mean that things are really bad.

I pulled away from Mum and stood up.

'I'm going to my room,' I said. 'I'm going to make Alice the very best "Get Well" card ever. Because she's going to get well. She has to.'

*   *   *

A while later the telephone rang.

I ran to the hall, but Mum got there before me, so I got to listen to one half of a conversation.

'Yes.'

'Oh.'

'Really?'

'I know.'

'I understand.'

'Yes.'

'Yes.'

'No.'

'Thanks.'

'Goodbye, and remember we're thinking of you all.'

Mum hung up and turned to me.

'Alice is stable,' she said.

'Stable' – I was sure I'd heard that word on hospital dramas, and I was pretty sure it was something good …

'What does stable mean?' I asked.

'It means Alice isn't getting any worse.'

'Does it mean she's getting better?'

Mum sighed. 'Well, not really. But it's early days yet. Try not to worry.'

That was like telling a river to try not to flow downhill, but I knew Mum was being kind, so I just did my best to smile.

'Peter will ring again in the morning,' said Mum.

Then she gave me a hug and went back into the kitchen, and I went back to my room to finish Alice's 'Get Well' card.

Chapter nineteen

When I woke in the morning, I stayed in bed, waiting for the phone to ring.

Then the door-bell rang instead.

I heard Mum answering it, and then I could hear Peter's voice in the hall.

Before I could do anything, Mum was at my bedroom door.

'Hurry up,' she said. 'Peter wants you to go and see Alice. The doctors think it might be good for her to hear your voice.'

I jumped out of bed, and threw on the tracksuit that had been on the floor of my bedroom. Then I pulled on my runners without even tying the laces, and I raced out to the hall.

'Ready?' asked Peter. He looked tired.

I nodded.

I followed Peter out to the car, and climbed in beside him.

'Is she awake yet?' I asked Peter as we drove off.

He shook his head.

'No. She's still … unconscious.'

He said the word slowly, almost like he couldn't bear the sound of it.

'Isn't that just like being asleep?' I asked.

'Well … sort of. It's like a very, very deep sleep. Alice hit her head somehow in the accident, and now the doctors say that her brain is just having a little rest. They think she might be able to hear us, though. And that's why we want you to talk to her. We know… well we know how much you two mean to each other, so the sound of your voice might make her want to wake up.'

I nodded, and then thought of something else.

'Do you know what happened to her? Do you know how she got hurt?'

He shook his head.

'No. It's still a complete mystery.'

I tried to smile.

'Alice likes mysteries,' I said, but then I was sorry, because I saw a small tear trickle down Peter's face. So I didn't say anything else until we got to the hospital.

*   *   *

Peter led the way to Alice's room.

'Try not to be afraid,' he said. 'There are lots of machines, and they're a bit scary at first, but you'll get used to them.'

I didn't answer. I hoped I wouldn't have to get used to them. I hoped Alice would be better soon and wouldn't need them. The machines could go to someone who was really sick.

Still, even after Peter's warning, I got a fright when I stepped in to the room. Alice was lying on a huge bed by the window. Her eyes were closed and her face was almost as white as the sheet she was lying on. There was a large purple bruise on her forehead. There were tubes coming out of both arms, and next to her there was a big machine that beeped loudly every few seconds.

She looked like she was dressed up as a ghost, for Halloween.

I wished she was just dressed up.

I wished she'd jump up and say 'boo' and we could have a laugh.

Slowly I looked around the room. I gasped when I saw Alice's mum, Veronica, who was sitting beside the bed. Veronica usually looks like a model with perfect hair and make-up and clothes that look like they'd been bought in a really expensive shop just minutes earlier. Even when Veronica is putting the bins out, she looks like she's dressed for a party.

Now Veronica looked like a wreck. She wasn't wearing any make-up. Her usually perfect nails were all broken and torn. Her hair was messier than my mum's on a bad day, and she was wearing clothes so untidy and mismatched that they made my dirty track-suit look like a princess's costume.

Alice's little brother Jamie was sitting on the floor, playing with some small toy cars.

I looked at Alice again, but nothing had changed.

I wished I could just walk away, and not be part of this horrible scene.

But I *was* part of it.

And I couldn't walk away.

Peter was smiling at me.

'Go and sit beside her,' he said. 'Talk to her.'

Veronica got up from her seat. She touched my shoulder.

'Sit there,' she said. 'And Megan ... thanks for coming.'

I sat down.

I reached out and touched Alice's hand. It was warm and dry. Her nails still had the pink nail varnish I'd painted on a few days earlier.

'Hi, Alice,' I said. My throat was dry, and my voice sounded too loud. It seemed to echo around the room.

Peter and Veronica smiled at me encouragingly.

'I'm sorry you're hurt, Alice,' I said. 'I know I didn't want you to go to France, but I wish you were there now. I wish you weren't here.'

Alice didn't respond. Her chest went up and down, but otherwise she didn't move. I had often seen her asleep, but I had never seen her so still.

'Domino came back,' I said. 'She just showed

up on my windowsill the other night. She was dirty and hungry, but she seems OK. I don't know what happened to her, but I think she got a fright. So maybe she won't run away again. I hope not anyway.'

It was strange talking to someone who seemed to be asleep.

It was very strange talking to Alice without her interrupting me, or laughing at something that I was saying.

But I knew I had to go on.

I told Alice that Mum was already going crazy cleaning the house for Linda's wedding, even though it was still ages away.

I told her that Rosie said she wanted her to hurry home.

I told her that I was making a card for her, but that it wasn't finished yet.

I told her all the things I could think of, but still Alice didn't move. She just lay there, white and still.

After a while, Peter tapped me on the shoulder.

'Your mum is here to bring you home,' he said.

I stood up and went outside to the corridor where Mum was waiting. I didn't want to go, but I didn't really want to stay either.

I just wanted everything to be all right again.

Chapter twenty

Mum let Domino sleep in my bed that night. In a way I was glad, because cuddling Domino is always nice. But it made me sad too, because I knew it meant that Mum was really

worried about Alice.

I thought about Alice all night long.

Alice doesn't even like sleeping late in the mornings – she's always afraid that she'll miss something exciting.

And now she'd been asleep for more than two days and two nights.

What was going to happen to her?

What if she never woke up again?

What if she just lay in that white bed, getting older and older, while the world went on without her?

*   *   *

The next day was Sunday, and in the morning Peter phoned again.

When Mum had finished talking to him, she came and looked in through my bedroom door.

'How's Alice?' I asked.

Mum shook her head slowly.

'I'm sorry, Megan,' she said. 'No change.'

*   *   *

I lay in bed, looking at the ceiling.

If only I hadn't made that stupid, stupid wish on Linda's ring. The wish might not have made any difference, but it was still making me feel very, very guilty.

Then I made a decision. I *had* to tell someone or I was going to go crazy.

I got dressed quickly, and ran into the kitchen.

'I'm calling over to Kellie's house for a while,' I said, and then I raced out the door before Mum could call me back and make me eat breakfast.

Luckily Kellie was at home. She had already heard that Alice was in hospital, and she listened patiently while I filled in the details for her. She cried a bit and she hugged me, and then we chatted about Alice for ages. Kellie was really, really nice, and did all she could to make me feel better.

I knew that, except for Alice, Kellie was the best friend I had ever had.

I also knew that I wasn't brave enough to tell her about my wish.

How could I tell her that?

How could I risk making her hate me?

So after a while, I told her I needed to do some jobs for Mum. Then we had one more hug, and I set off for home.

* * *

I walked very slowly.

I didn't want to be at home.

I didn't want to be anywhere.

I walked with my hands in my pockets and my head down, kicking a small stone along in front of me. I watched without much interest as it rattled along the footpath.

Suddenly I felt angry with myself, and I kicked the stone as hard as I could. It bounced off a wall, and then whacked into the legs of someone who was walking towards me.

I didn't dare to look up.

'Omigod,' I muttered. 'I'm really sorry. I didn't mean— '

'Hey, Megan,' said a familiar voice. 'I see you're still getting into trouble.'

I looked up.

'Marcus!' I said. 'What are you doing here?'

'I'm home for the weekend,' he said.

Then he gave me a huge smile, and I suddenly realised that I was very glad to see him.

'How's boarding school?' I asked.

He shrugged. 'It's not too bad. You'd be proud of me. I wear my uniform every day. And I don't get into trouble ... well not too much trouble anyway.'

I had to laugh.

'I'm glad,' I said. 'I'm really glad.'

'And what about you?' he asked. 'How are you?'

'I'm fine,' I said. 'But Alice ......'

'Alice what?'

I told him about Alice's accident.

Marcus and Alice had never been friends, but that didn't seem to matter now. He listened like he really cared.

'Poor Alice,' he said, when I was finished. 'You must be really worried about her.'

I nodded, and then there was a silence.

Did I dare to tell Marcus about my wish?

Would he think I was totally evil?

But last year he'd done loads of bad stuff. Did that mean he'd be able to understand this one bad thing that I had done?

Or would he just laugh at me, and rush back to his boarding school to tell all his new friends about this crazy superstitious girl he knew in Limerick?

I made a quick decision. Then I took a deep breath, and started to talk.

'There was this competition ...' I began. Marcus listened carefully until I came to the end of my tale, '.... so you see, I never wanted Alice to go to France, and then I made that stupid wish, and then she had the accident, and it's all my fault. The whole thing is my fault.'

I stopped talking and waited for Marcus to start laughing.

I waited and waited, but he didn't laugh. He didn't even smile. Then he did something very strange. Very slowly he put first one hand and then the other on my shoulders. Before I could think too much about how weird this was, he leaned forwards and hugged me tightly.

'Poor, Megan,' he said. 'Poor, poor Megan.'

Being hugged by Marcus was nice, but soon I started to feel embarrassed.

I pulled away. I knew that I was blushing, but I didn't feel too bad when I saw that Marcus's face was starting to go red too.

He put his hand up and pushed his hair out of his eyes.

'Don't feel guilty, Megan,' he said. 'It's not your fault. I know it's not your fault.'

'How do you know?' I asked.

'Because if wishing things made them happen, my life would be different now. I'd live in a huge house with a swimming pool and a soccer pitch in the back garden. I'd have a big brother, and a little brother and loads of sisters.' He hesitated and then finished in a low voice. 'And if wishing things made them happen, my mum would still be alive.'

Now it was my turn to put my hand on his shoulder.

'I'm sorry,' I said.

He shrugged.

'It's OK. But just hear what I'm saying. Of course you didn't want Alice to go away to France. She's your best friend, so that's only natural. Wanting to be with your best friend isn't a crime. And that wish you made – well that was just a stupid wish, and it doesn't count for anything. Do you believe me?'

He put his hands on my arms and squeezed them tightly, and for one second I felt afraid.

Then he dropped his hands to his sides, and smiled. 'When you see Alice, tell her I hope she gets better soon, OK?'

I nodded. 'OK. Oh, and Marcus …'

He was already walking away, but he stopped and turned back to face me.

'What?'

'When you're home for the weekend again, text me. Maybe we can meet up. You and me and my friends. Maybe we could go to the cinema or something.'

He smiled.

'I'd like that,' he said.

And then he turned again and walked away.

Chapter twenty-one

After lunch, Peter called to bring me to the hospital.

Once again, Jamie was playing with his cars on the floor.

Alice was still lying on the bed with her eyes closed. She still looked pale and sick and not really like herself at all.

Nothing had changed except that Veronica looked even untidier than she had the day before. When she saw me, she stood up and moved over to the corner of the room.

'Why don't you go to get something

to eat now that Megan's here?' asked Peter. 'If you don't eat, you're going to get sick too.'

But Veronica just shook her head.

'I don't care if I get sick,' she said. 'I can't leave. I'm Alice's mum. I have to be here when she wakes up.'

Peter didn't argue. He looked too tired to argue.

I sat down beside Alice. I touched her hand, and then stopped when I realised I was patting her like she was a puppy.

'Hi Alice,' I said. 'We're all dying to know what happened to you. It's a real mystery. I wish you'd wake up and tell us.'

There was no response, but by now I'd learned not to expect one. I just wondered what I was supposed to say next.

I put my hand into my pocket, and felt a sudden rush of relief when my fingers touched my phone.

'All your friends say "hi",' I said. 'They've been texting me all morning. There are messages from Grace and Louise and Kellie and Josh, and loads of other people. I'll read them out to you.'

I switched on my phone and read out all the messages. Alice didn't even blink.

I tried again.

'Linda phoned Mum this morning. She was very sorry when she heard about your accident. She and Luka said you're to get better soon. They are all excited about their wedding. It's going to be sooo much fun.'

Alice had been so excited when I told her about the wedding, but now she lay there without moving. I might as well have been talking about maths problems.

I suddenly remembered a word that Mr Dunne had taught us in English class. 'Monologue,' he had said. 'It's when one character in a play speaks for along time, with no interruption from anyone else.'

Now, for the first time, I understood what he meant.

I held back my tears, and continued my monologue.

'Oh, and guess who I met this morning?'

I felt stupid when I remembered that Alice wasn't in a position to guess anything.

So I answered for her.

'I met Marcus this morning. I know you never liked him very much, but that's because you never got to know him properly. Maybe when you're better we can meet up with him and you can see that he's really very nice.'

I was running out of things to say.

My monologue had ground to a halt.

I looked around the room. Peter and Veronica smiled at me, but didn't say anything. Jamie was making car noises that were so loud and horrible that I knew Alice would tell him to shut up – if only she could.

It was totally weird. I missed Alice so much it was giving me a pain in my chest. And yet she was only half a metre away from me. How could that be?

I got up and walked over to the window. It was a cold, sunny day. A man was walking on the footpath outside. A sudden gust of wind blew his hat into the air. He ran after it, but every time he came close, it blew out of his reach.

'Look, Al…..' I began, before I remembered.

I pressed my face to the window, so no one could see my tears.

Then I heard one word.

'Domino.'

Was that …?

Could it be …?

I spun around quickly.

Veronica and Peter were beside the bed, where Alice was lying with her eyes open, looking slightly surprised.

'Hey, I'm trying to play here,' said Jamie, but no one took any notice.

I raced over to the bed.

'Megan?' said Alice, looking even more surprised than before.

By now Veronica was crying big loud sobs, and Peter was frantically ringing the bell over Alice's bed.

Jamie stood up and folded his arms.

'I don't get it,' he said to Veronica. 'Before, you were crying because Alice was asleep, and now she's awake and you're still not happy.'

At that Veronica started to laugh through her tears. She reached out to hug Jamie, and Peter bent down hugged Alice, and I stepped away to let them enjoy their happy moment.

And I did my own small dance of happiness over by the window.

My best friend was back.

Chapter twenty-two

After that, lots of nurses and doctors came in.

Some of them looked into Alice's eyes. Some of them asked her stupid questions like what was her name, and when was her birthday. They seemed pleased when she gave them the right answers. One nurse patted Alice's head, and said, 'Clever girl.'

For a second I felt really angry. She was thirteen years old – a teen-ager – so why were they treating her like she was a little baby?

Then one of the doctors took

Peter and Veronica aside, and they whispered together for a while. Veronica who had stopped crying, suddenly started again, even louder than before.

I felt a sudden stab of fear. Then I saw that Peter was smiling, and I realised that Veronica was crying happy tears. I could understand why Jamie was so confused.

Soon there was only one nurse left in the room. She straightened Alice's sheets, and checked the machine that was still beeping next to her bed.

Then she looked at Peter, Veronica, Jamie and me.

'Don't upset the patient,' she said. 'Don't ask her about her accident. There will be time enough for that tomorrow, when she's feeling better. OK?'

We all nodded, and the nurse continued. 'And after five minutes you'll have to go away. Alice needs to rest.'

It seemed to me that Alice had done nothing except rest for the past few days, but the nurse didn't look like the type to involve in that kind of argument, so I didn't say this.

We all clustered around the bed. Now that Alice was awake, I wondered if I should warn her that she might drown in her mother's tears.

'Can I talk to her?' I said.

Peter and Veronica nodded.

'Hi, Alice,' I said, feeling suddenly shy.

'Hi, Meg,' said Alice in a weak, hoarse voice. Suddenly I remembered something.

'When you woke up, you said "Domino". Were you dreaming about her? I didn't think you liked cats enough to dream about them.'

Alice shook her head, then stopped and put her hand to her bruised forehead.

'No,' she said. 'I wasn't dreaming about Domino. But I found her. I saved her.'

What was she talking about?

Was she still half asleep?

I looked at Peter and Veronica.

Veronica was pulling yet another tissue from her pocket, and using it to wipe her eyes. Peter shrugged as if to say he had no idea what his daughter was talking about either.

I remembered that we weren't supposed to be upsetting Alice or talking about her accident.

'Er … right,' I said. 'Whatever.'

'*Really*,' said Alice. 'I found Domino and saved her.'

'I'm sorry, Alice,' I said, 'but I don't understand.'

Alice didn't say anything for a minute. Then she spoke quickly, in a funny whispery kind of voice.

'I was just going to get ready for bed, and I was thinking about how sad you were because Domino was missing. And then I remembered that when you and me and Kellie and the others did the big search, none of us went down Shelbourne Road, and that was stupid because there are so many big houses there, with big gardens where Domino could get lost. So I was going to call for you and ask you to come with me, but I thought your mum would be cross with me for calling so late. So I just decided to go on my own, for a quick look. I walked down Shelbourne Road, calling Domino's name, and then I heard a tiny weak miaow. At first I thought I had imagined it, and then I heard it again. I looked up, and I saw that Domino was up a tree, just near the footpath. I called and called her, but she wouldn't come down. She just kept saying this tiny little miaow, and you know I don't like cats all that much, but I felt really sorry for her. I couldn't just go away and leave her there, and there was no one else around to help. So I decided to climb up the tree, and when I got up, I saw that Domino's collar was caught in a branch, and that's why she couldn't get down. So I climbed right up next to her, and freed her collar. I tried to pick her up, but she wriggled out of my arms, and ran down the tree. I saw her racing along the footpath towards your house, as fast as anything. And ......'

Alice stopped talking. She looked weak and tired.

'And what?' prompted Peter.

Alice shook her head slowly.

'And I can't remember any more after that.'

She lay back on her pillows and breathed deeply, like she'd just run a marathon or something.

'You must have fallen out of the tree,' said Peter.

'Cool,' said Jamie.

'Oh, Alice, you only got hurt because you saved Domino,' I said. 'She came home straight away, and I never knew how. Thanks, Alice, but I'm so sorry that you got hurt.'

No one said anything for a minute. We all had lots to think about.

'How did I get here?' asked Alice after a while.

'Luckily, you must have screamed while you were falling,' said Peter. 'And a man heard you and called an ambulance. The ambulance brought you to hospital and you've been here ever since.'

Alice looked puzzled.

'Ever since?' she said.

'That was on Thursday night. It's Sunday now,' said Peter gently.

'I've lost nearly three days,' said Alice.

I had a sudden thought.

'You always give me a hard time just because you're two days older than me, but maybe now I've caught up,' I said. 'Maybe I'm a day older than you now.'

Alice gave a small, weak smile.

'No way,' she said.

Just then the nurse came back into the room.

'I can't believe you're all still here,' she said. 'Off you go, the whole lot of you, and let this girl get some sleep.'

Peter and Veronica kissed Alice.

'We'll be right outside,' said Veronica. 'Just call if you need us.'

I gave Alice a small hug, and then we all left the room.

The nurse followed us, muttering crossly, but I didn't care. She could mutter all she liked.

Alice was awake, and nothing else mattered.

Chapter twenty-three

When I got to school the next day, everyone crowded around me, pushing and shoving and asking endless questions. They had all heard that Alice had had an accident, but except for Kellie, no one knew exactly how she was, or what had happened to her.

At first it was OK. I felt kind of important, because I was the one who knew the stuff that everyone else was desperate to find out.

Very soon after I arrived at school though, I was fed up of telling people the story.

I was a bit embarrassed when I told about how Alice got hurt trying to save Domino. Some kids laughed, and some people thought it was stupid getting hurt just to save a cat.

'Don't cats have nine lives?' asked Michael who thinks he's really clever. 'Alice has only one, so she should have been more careful.

Only Kellie seemed to understand how I felt. She put her arm around me.

'Don't feel guilty, Megan,' she said. 'It's not your fault. Everyone knows that Alice is a dare-devil. I bet she didn't think twice about climbing up that tree. I'm a total chicken, but I'd have done it too. I couldn't bear to see a little kitty in trouble.'

I knew she was right. Even if I had been standing there with Alice, screaming at her not to climb the tree, she still would have done it.

Just then Grace and Louise came along. The four of us hugged. I'd been texting them all weekend, but now they wanted the details of the accident, so I had to go back to the beginning and tell the whole story all over again.

'What about France?' asked Grace as soon as I was finished. 'Is Alice still allowed to go?'

I shook my head.

'No. She's going to be in hospital until the weekend at least, and the doctors said that even after that she won't be well enough to travel for a while. Her dad's coming to talk to Mrs Kingston today, to see if the prize can be given to someone else.'

Grace grinned.

'It'll be my friend Hannah. She came second in the competition, so she'll have to get the chance to go to France now, the lucky thing. I'm going to go and find her, and tell her. She'll be sorry that Alice is hurt, but I know she'll be totally excited about going to France.'

Grace and Louise ran off, and Kellie and I got

our books ready for the first class. For once in my life, I was glad to be sitting in a classroom – it was a relief not to be the centre of attention for a while.

* * *

After school I went to see Alice in hospital. She was still pale, but she was sitting up in bed. She gave a small, tired smile when she saw me.

'Hi, Meg,' she said. 'Anything exciting happening?'

What was I supposed to say to that?

Something exciting should be happening.

Alice should be on her first day in boarding school in France. She should be making a whole heap of new friends, and having the time of her life.

But because of my cat (the cat that Alice had never even liked very much), her trip was ruined.

Alice was waiting for an answer. I wondered if

I'd be brave enough to tell her about Hannah going to France in her place.

Then she rescued me.

'Dad says someone is going to France in my place. I suppose it's going to be Hannah?'

I nodded.

'Yes. It's all sorted. She's going next week. I'm sorry, Al,' I said. 'Really I am.'

Alice shrugged.

'It's OK,' she said. 'I don't mind that much really.'

She was lying, and I could see that she knew that I knew that she was lying.

But she didn't seem to care.

'There's good news too,' I said suddenly. 'Hannah's going to give you the MP3 player she won in the competition. She told me she hasn't even used it yet.'

'Oh,' said Alice.

Then I realised how stupid I was being. Alice

had just lost the chance of a big trip to France. How was an MP3 player supposed to make up for that? (Especially as Alice had already got the best one you can buy for Christmas.)

I stayed for another twenty minutes. For the first time in our lives, Alice and I struggled for things to talk about, and when a nurse came in and said I had to go, I was glad. I gave Alice a hug, promised to come back the next day, and then I left.

*   *   *

Alice was in hospital for four more days, and each day I visited her.

Each day was worse than the one before.

No matter how hard I tried to cheer her up, Alice was too sad and too quiet.

It was like my best friend had vanished, to be replaced by a paler shadow of herself.

On the day before Alice was due to go home, I

met Veronica as I came out of Alice's room.

Veronica was back to normal, with perfect hair, perfect nails, and totally perfect clothes. I thought differently about her these days – now that I knew there was a real, loving mum hidden inside under all the perfection.

'Megan, dear,' said Veronica now. 'It is so sweet of you to visit Alice every day like this.'
I shrugged.

'That's OK. Alice is my friend. I like visiting her.'

Veronica looked closely at me.

Could she see through me?

Could she tell that I was lying?

Veronica took my arm.

'Come and sit down and talk to me,' she said, pulling me towards a seat a little way along the corridor.

I felt a sudden urge to run away – very fast.

Alice got hurt saving my cat, and now

Veronica could see that I hated visiting her in hospital.

What mother could forgive a girl for that?

Was I going to get my eyes scratched out by the most beautiful long nails in Limerick?

We both sat down.

I looked along the corridor, wondering if some nice doctor might come along to rescue me.

Would I need a doctor by the time Veronica was finished with me?

'I think you find visiting Alice a bit difficult,' said Veronica.

I gulped.

Should I lie?

Was there any point in lying, since Veronica had obviously copped on to the truth?

'Er … not really … well … maybe … er ……
yes …… just a little bit,' I muttered.

I waited for Veronica to attack, but she didn't. She just gave a small, sad smile.

'Alice isn't herself yet,' she said. 'The doctors say that's only to be expected after an injury like the one she's had. And besides, her leg is hurting.'

I nodded, and Veronica continued. 'And we mustn't forget that she's disappointed about not going to France.'

I nodded again, not knowing what to say.

'Anyway,' said Veronica brightly. 'Alice is going home tomorrow, and everything will be fine then. Just you wait and see.'

I *so* wasn't going to argue with Veronica.

So I nodded one more time.

'Yes,' I said. 'Let's just wait and see.'

Chapter twenty-four

A week later Alice was back at school. She wasn't well enough to walk all the way, so her dad drove her. I travelled with them. When we got to the school, I jumped out of the car first, carrying my bag and Alice's.

Everyone stared as Alice slowly climbed out of the car and balanced herself on the one crutch she needed to walk.

Michael, the loud stupid boy in our year, pushed to the front of the crowd.

'Hey, welcome back, Hopalong,' he called.

I stared at

Alice, waiting for a response. The old Alice would have grabbed Michael and threatened to knock his head off with her crutch. For a moment nothing happened, then Alice put her head down, like she hadn't heard a single, stupid word.

'That's totally mean,' I said to Michael.

He shrugged.

'So what do you plan to do about it?'

I hesitated. Alice should know what to do next. She never lets people get away with being mean.

But Alice was standing with her head down, fiddling with the handle of her crutch.

I walked away from Michael, and back towards Alice.

'He's just an idiot,' I said.

'Whatever,' said Alice in a dull voice.

I suddenly felt angry.

'You shouldn't listen to idiots like Michael.'

But Alice was already walking away.

'Come on, Megan,' she said, 'or we'll be late for class.'

I felt like crying.

Alice was back.

And yet she wasn't.

*   *   *

Before the accident, Alice, Grace, Louise, Kellie and I used to spend all of our lunch and breaktimes together. We'd go to the canteen and eat our food as quickly as we could. Then the five of us would go outside. We'd walk around the school grounds, laughing and talking about nothing.

Now, though, everything was different. Because of her sore leg, Alice had to stay inside. Because I was her best friend, I was allowed to stay with her.

It should have been my idea of heaven. Alice

hadn't gone to France, and now I was getting to spend loads of time with her, with no one else around, no one else competing for her attention.

For the first time ever, I understood what Mum often says – be careful what you wish for.

It was awful.

Alice never laughed, and she rarely smiled.

Every day I struggled to make conversation. No matter what I said, Alice always answered politely, without seeming very interested.

We were like two, not very exciting, strangers at a bus-stop.

Sometimes this made me feel like running home and crying until I had no tears left.

Sometimes it made me feel that I'd love to pick Alice up and shake her.

But most days I struggled on, wishing that I was outside in the fresh air with Grace, Louise and Kellie.

The scariest thing was that Alice didn't seem to

notice that she was different to before.

'Is your leg very sore?' I'd ask, or 'Are you very disappointed that you didn't get to go to France?'

And Alice would just shrug, and say, 'It doesn't matter.'

And I'd sit there, and wonder what to say next.

*   *   *

It seemed like a very long week, and I was glad when Friday, Home Ec day, came along.

Grace, Alice and I walked along the corridor to the cookery room.

'I'm not sure that I can face cooking today,' I said. 'Mum's gone even more crazy than usual. She's practising new dishes to serve for Linda's wedding.'

'Isn't that a good thing?' asked Grace.

I shook my head.

'Obviously you don't know my mum very well. Dinner times in our house were bad enough when we knew what to expect.'

Grace laughed.

'Megan, you are so funny sometimes.'

I felt pleased, and turned to see if Alice was laughing. She wasn't of course. She just had her usual blank expression on her face.

'I bet Miss Leonard is really happy that you didn't go to France after all,' I said to Alice.

'Whatever,' she said.

It felt like the hundredth time that day that she'd said, 'whatever' and I felt like punching her.

But I had a horrible feeling that if I did punch her, she'd just give me the same blank look, and say 'whatever' one more time.

Grace tried to help.

'I've brought the ingredients for quiche,' she said, 'but you can cook if you like, Alice.'

For one moment I felt hopeful. So many things can go wrong when you are making quiche. If Alice started to break eggs, and measure out flour, maybe she'd turn back into the old

Alice. Maybe she'd wreck the cookery room. Maybe Miss Leonard's nightmare would turn out to be my dream come true.

But Alice just shook her head.

'Thanks, Grace,' she said, 'but I'm a bit tired, today. You and Megan can cook. I'll just watch.'

I felt awful, but I tried to be positive – Alice had just spoken more than one full sentence, and she hadn't used the word 'whatever' once.

Chapter twenty-five

The next few weeks passed very slowly. Alice never wanted to come to my house after school, and she never invited me to her place. When she wasn't at school, she just sat at home.

In the beginning I used to ask her to do stuff with me, but after a while, I stopped. I got tired of hearing Alice say 'no' to everything I suggested.

Every day felt like a month, as I hung out with my best friend's shadow, wondering if the real Alice was ever going to come back.

And then one day, when I was almost giving up hope of Alice ever getting back to normal, it looked like things were going to change.

It was lunchtime and Alice and I were sitting inside as usual. She didn't need a crutch any more, but she still limped a bit. The doctors said it would be another few weeks before her leg was fully back to normal.

At last the bell rang to let us know that it was time to go back to class.

'Let's go,' I said, trying not to show how relieved I was. 'Do you want me to give you a hand with your books?'

Alice didn't move.

'Let's skip class,' she said.

I gulped. I'd never skipped class before.

What if we got caught?

We'd be in heaps of trouble.

And my next class was Geography with Mr Spillane. He never misses anything.

'I don't know,' I began. 'I—'

'Come on,' said Alice. '*Please*, Megan.'

I grinned. OK, so I was terrified, but if Alice wanted to skip class, that was a good sign.

Wasn't it?

We found an empty room next to the science lab. We went in, closed the door and sat down.

Now what?

Was this supposed to be fun?

Alice was gazing through the window, like the recycling bin outside was the most wonderful, exciting thing she had ever seen.

'I'm supposed to be in Geography now,' I said after a while. 'I suppose you're missing Business Studies. I know how you hate it.'

Alice spoke in the dreamy voice that I was getting to know so well and hate so much.

'No,' she said. 'I'm not missing Business. I'm supposed to be at PE.'

'But you love—' I began, before Alice interrupted me.

'I *don't* love PE,' she said fiercely. 'I hate it. I hate every single moment of it.'

'But Miss Ryan is so nice,' I began. 'Surely she—'

'That's the trouble,' said Alice. 'Miss Ryan is very nice. She's much *too* nice. She lets me keep score when we play indoor soccer. And if we're not playing soccer, she invents sitting-down games just so I can join in. She always asks me how I am, and she seems to care about the answer. She's totally nice.'

'And the problem is?'

'I don't want to be the girl in the corner who the teachers are nice to. I want to be the girl in the middle of the gym, scoring goals.'

'But your leg is going to get better,' I said.

'The doctors said so.'

Suddenly Alice wasn't fierce any more.

'It's not just my leg, though, is it?' she asked.

'What do you mean?' I asked, knowing exactly what she meant.

She stared at me like she wanted to see inside my brain.

'Tell me the truth, Megan,' she said. 'What do you think is wrong with me?'

I started to think of half-answers – ways to tell her that nothing was wrong. But then I found that I couldn't do it. Alice was my friend. It was time to tell her the truth.

I thought for a long time, and then I took a deep breath.

'You're almost the same as before,' I began, 'but not quite. It's like … it's like you're a jigsaw puzzle, and there's one piece missing. And without that single piece, nothing seems right any more. It's like the sparkly bit, the bit that makes you different to everyone else – that bit's not there any more.'

At first Alice smiled.

'That's exactly how I feel,' she said. 'You're really good at explaining things.'

I smiled back at her, but my smile faded quickly as Alice started to cry.

'Help me, Megan,' she said through her tears. 'Please help me to get better.'

I was close to tears too.

How could I have let my best friend down like this?

I'd been so busy missing Alice, it had never occurred to me that she might be missing herself.

I hugged her for a long time. Alice clung on to me like she was lost at sea, and I was the only person who could save her from drowning.

I had to do something, but I had no idea what to do.

I wasn't a doctor.

How was I supposed to help her to get better?

At last I let her go. For the first time, I noticed how thin and tired she looked.

'Maybe you just need to be patient,' I said.

'I don't want to be patient,' said Alice, stamping her good foot.

I giggled.

'That's a start I suppose,' I said. 'That's more like the Alice I used to know.'

She sighed.

'It's not so hard when I'm here with you. But when everyone else is around, it's like I don't feel like trying any more. I don't feel like going out shopping or to the cinema or anything. I wouldn't even go to school, except that Mum and Dad insist – and I'm too tired to argue with them. All I want to do is stay at home, where I'm safe and warm.'

Then I had an idea.

'Maybe you need to force yourself,' I said.

'Maybe you need to make yourself do stuff, even if you don't want to do it. And then if you do one thing, and it turns out OK, you'll be brave enough to do other stuff. And then, before you know it, you'll be back to normal. What do you think?'

Alice was quiet for a long time.

Had I offended her?

Or had she fallen asleep?

At last she spoke.

'Like force myself to do what?'

Why did I always get the hard questions?

As I was struggling to find an answer, the bell rang for the beginning of the next class.

'I've absolutely got to go,' I said. 'I'm not brave enough to miss two classes in a row.'

To my relief, Alice didn't argue. We gathered up our books, and went our separate ways along the corridor.

Just then Kellie came along.

'Where were you?' she said to me.

'I, er …,' I began. 'I just had to do something.'

'With Alice?'

I nodded.

Kellie smiled.

'I guessed it was something like that. But don't worry. I covered for you. I told Mr Spillane that you were doing a job for one of the other teachers.'

I smiled. Kellie was a good friend.

'Back in a sec,' I said. 'I forgot something!'

Then I turned and ran after Alice, catching her just before she got to her next class.

'I won't let you down,' I said. 'I'll think of a plan, I promise.'

Alice gave me a quick hug.

'Thanks, Megan,' she said.

Then she went in to her class.

Chapter twenty-six

For the next few classes, I struggled for an answer.

I had to think of some kind of challenge for Alice.

But if I picked something too hard, she'd just refuse to do it.

And if I picked something too easy, she'd know I was treating her like a baby,

and she'd refuse as well.

And then, in the middle of a totally boring history class, the perfect answer came to me.

I met Alice as she

came out of her last class.

'It's all sorted,' I said.

She looked at me like I was crazy.

'Your first proper trip into the outside world,' I said.

'Oh, that,' said Alice, without much interest.

I continued anyway.

'Linda's coming to Limerick on Saturday, to buy her wedding dress. Mum and Rosie and I are going with her. We're all going in to O'Donnell's. They have heaps of beautiful dresses there. You can come with us. You love helping people to pick out nice clothes.'

Alice shook her head.

'I don't think so. That's a family kind of thing. I'd only be in the way.'

I was ready for this.

'You *have* to come,' I said. 'Linda's really bad at making decisions. Mum will try to force her to buy something totally gross, and Rosie will agree with Mum, because that's what she always does. I won't be able to stand up to them all on my own. I need you to be on my side. I need you to help me to save Linda from a fashion disaster.'

Alice still didn't look very excited.

'You know I still can't walk very far,' she said.

I grinned. This one was easy.

'That doesn't matter. You'll hardly have to walk at all. Dad will drive us there and pick us up when we're finished. Now, any more excuses?'

Alice was quiet for a while. Then she smiled.

'I should do this, shouldn't I?'

I nodded.

'Yes, you should do this.'

Now Alice smiled an even bigger smile.

'Then I will do it,' she said. 'You were right, Megan. I've got to be brave.'

* * *

Linda arrived early on Saturday, and after a quick

snack of sugar-free oatmeal cookies, washed down with a big mug of dandelion coffee, we were ready to go. Rosie was all excited, like we were going on a big expedition, instead of just in to town. I was excited too, though. I was looking forward to helping Linda to choose a wedding dress, but more than that, I was looking forward to doing something fun with Alice at last.

'You all get in the car,' I said. 'I'll go and call for Alice. I've told her to be ready.'

It took ages for Alice to answer the door, and when she did, I was not happy to see that she was still in her pyjamas.

'Alice,' I said. 'You're supposed to be ready. Get dressed quickly. Everyone's waiting.'

Alice put her head down.

'I'm not going with you.'

'But you have to,' I protested.

Alice shook her head.

'I'm sorry, Megan. I'm a bit tired this morning.'

I couldn't believe what I was hearing.

'We'll only be gone for an hour. It'll be fun. We'll choose the dress, and then Linda's taking us all for hot chocolate and … you promised, remember? You promised me that you'd come out with us today.'

'I know I promised, Megan. And I'm sorry, but now I'm not coming. Anyway, I want to tidy my bookshelf. I've been meaning to do it for ages. I'm actually looking forward to getting started.'

Suddenly I felt angry. Alice had never willingly tidied a bookshelf in her whole life.

Alice folded her arms and stared at me.

And then I realised something strange.

Alice had changed an awful lot since her accident.

She wasn't daring any more.

She wasn't funny any more.

She wasn't witty, or sparkly or lively any more.

But she had somehow managed to hold on to

the one trait that really, really annoyed me – she was just as stubborn as ever.

I could have argued with Alice, but there was no point. I'd have done just as well arguing with the front door. She wasn't going to change her mind and there wasn't a single thing I could do about it.

I started to walk away.

'I'm really, really sorry, Megan,' she said to my back. 'I promise I'll do something with you next week.'

Don't bother, I felt like shouting back.

But I didn't.

I just kept walking.

* * *

The trip to town should have been totally fun.

We went in to O'Donnell's and when we explained what we wanted, the assistant went all soppy and misty-eyed.

'A wedding dress,' she sighed. 'How romantic. I remember my own wedding day like it was yesterday.'

That set Mum off, and the two of them spent twenty minutes going on and on about how wonderful their own wedding days were. In the end, Linda had to interrupt them.

'Er … about *my* wedding dress,' she began.

Mum went red.

'Sorry, Linda,' she said. 'I get so carried away sometimes.'

'Do you want to talk about it?' I said, and everyone laughed.

The assistant was staring at Linda.

'We have many, many dresses here,' she said in the end. 'But I think I know exactly which one would be right for you. It only came in this morning, and I didn't have a chance to put it on display yet.'

Before anyone could say anything, the

assistant vanished into a back room of the shop. When she came back, she was carrying a dress. It was made of pale blue silk, with little ruffles on the sleeves, and tiny blue pearls all along the neck-line. It was the most beautiful dress I had ever seen.

Linda took the dress from the assistant and went in to the changing room. When she came out there was a short silence, and then everyone spoke at once.

'It's totally gorgeous,' I said.

'It's perfect,' Mum said.

'It's absolutely delightful,' the assistant said.

'You look like a princess,' Rosie said.

'Luka is going to love it,' said Linda. 'Did I mention that he loves the colour blue?'

'Only about a hundred times,' said Mum, and everyone laughed again.

After Linda had paid for the dress, she took us to a café, as she had promised. Mum had organic green tea, and didn't make too much of a fuss when Linda bought huge mugs of hot chocolate with marshmallows for Rosie and me.

Rosie absolutely loves marshmallows. She kept squeezing them with her fingers.

'They feel like pillows,' she said.

Linda grinned at her, and when Mum went to the toilet, she got another handful of marshmallows and put them into Rosie's drink.

Rosie looked like she was going to fall off her stool she was so excited.

'I'm a happy, happy girl,' she sang.

Linda hugged her.

'I'm a happy girl too,' she said. 'What about you, Megan?'

I didn't answer.

How could I be happy, when my best friend in the whole world was at home tidying her bookshelf?

And enjoying it.

Chapter twenty-seven

The next day Alice called over with a tiny box of chocolates in her hand.

'They're for you, Megan,' she said. 'To say sorry about yesterday.'

I took the box from her. I love chocolates, but I'd have given all the chocolates in the world, just to see Alice laugh like she used to.

'Thanks,' I said. 'Do you want to come in

for a while?'

'No, I …' began Alice and then she hesitated.

If she mentioned something stupid like tidying a bookshelf, I didn't know if I could stop myself from punching her.

Then Alice started to speak again.

'Actually, I will come in. Thanks.'

I smiled. It was only a small step, but it was a step in the right direction.

*   *   *

Half an hour later, I was totally bored. Alice had said 'whatever' to everything I suggested, so we'd ended up playing Monopoly. I was winning and Alice wasn't even cheating to catch up. It was no fun at all.

I was glad when Mum came in and interrupted us.

'I'm trying a new dish tonight,' she said. 'And if it's nice, I'll cook it for Linda's wedding.'

'Muuuum,' I moaned. 'Isn't there a law against using your family as guinea pigs?'

She ignored me.

'I've run out of lentils,' she said. 'And I need loads because I'm making cabbage rolls stuffed with couscous and lentils.'

I groaned as loudly as I could, and Mum ignored me again.

'So I want you to go to the shop for me please. I'm sure Alice would like to go with you.'

'I ... ,' began Alice.

I didn't let her finish.

'Of course she'd like to come with me,' I said.

Alice stood up, and we followed Mum into the hall.

Mum handed me the money, and a shopping bag.

'And here,' she said. 'Put this on. It's cold outside.'

She was holding out what looked like a giant,

over-fed worm. It was the scarf she had knitted me for my thirteenth birthday. This had to be the ugliest scarf in the history of the world. I was forever hiding it, but no matter what hiding place I found, it always turned up again. Sometimes I thought that it must crawl out, looking for food.

I took the scarf, knowing that Mum wouldn't give up until it was firmly wrapped around my neck.

Was this my punishment for being cheeky to her?

Alice and I set off.

'Remind me to take this scarf off as soon as we get around the corner,' I said. 'I look like I'm being strangled by a prehistoric swamp creature.'

Alice didn't even laugh. She just gave that new, vague, Alice-shrug, that was starting to drive me crazy.

Then, before we got to the first corner, I saw

something that made my stomach turn over and over, making me suddenly feel sick and dizzy.

It was walking towards us.

It was flicking its blonde hair.

It was the one and only …… Melissa.

Meeting Melissa at any time was a pain, but meeting her while I was wearing a gross, hand-knitted scarf was a total disaster.

I wondered if I could take the scarf off, and fling it into a hedge, but it was too late. Melissa had seen us.

Phew, at least Alice is with me, I thought, before I remembered that it was the old Alice that I needed.

Melissa-hating was once our favourite hobby, and I could always rely on Alice to rescue me when Melissa was mean.

But that was before.

I nudged Alice.

'Look who's coming,' I said.

Alice looked up.

'Oh,' she said, like it was the postman or the milkman or someone boring like that.

Soon Melissa was right next to us.

'Hi Alice, hi Megan,' she said.

'Hi Melissa,' we chorused.

Suddenly Melissa put her hand over her mouth, in a big fake show of trying to stop laughing.

'Omigod,' she said. 'Megan, whatever is that *thing* around your neck? It looks like it's trying to kill you.'

I could feel my face going red. I knew that as soon as I got home, I'd be able to think of loads of clever answers, but by then it would be too late.

Melissa wasn't finished.

'I suppose your mum knitted that … thing … for you,' she sneered. 'Do you have to keep it in a special locked box, so it won't escape in the middle of the night and eat your whole family?'

I started to feel all hot and shivery. I soooo wanted to stand up to Melissa, but I couldn't think of how to do that. I opened my mouth, but no words came out to help me.

Then I noticed a small movement beside me. Alice was folding her arms, and drawing herself up until she was taller than usual. She narrowed her eyes as she stared at Melissa.

'Can *your* mum knit?' she asked sweetly.

Melissa shook her head.

'She's not a *total* loser. Of course she can't *knit*.'

Alice smiled.

'Pity,' she said. 'Because if your mum *could* knit, she could knit a big bag to go over your head, so none of us would have to hurt our eyes by looking at your ugly face.'

Melissa opened her mouth and made a pathetic squeaky noise that made no sense. She never had been very good at taking her own medicine.

I looked at Alice. She was grinning madly, with that old Alice sparkle I'd thought had gone forever.

I turned around and gave her a huge hug.

'Oh, Alice,' I cried. 'I've missed you so much.'

I let her go and she stared at me.

'Oh, Megan,' she said. 'I think you're losing it.'

But she was smiling, and I knew she understood what I meant.

Melissa was starting to get over her shock.

'You're both crazy,' she said. Then with a flick of her blonde hair, she walked past us.

On a sudden impulse, I raced after her.

'Hey, Melissa,' I said, as soon as I drew level with her.

She stopped walking and turned to face me. 'What?' she said.

I stepped forwards and gave her a huge hug.

'Thanks, Melissa,' I said.

Melissa pulled away, like I was some disease

she didn't want to catch. 'What on earth was that for?' she asked.

I just laughed. 'You wouldn't understand,' I said, and then I ran back to my friend, and arm in arm we continued our journey to the shop.

Chapter twenty-eight

After that, things began to get slowly better. Sometimes Alice was tired, and didn't have the energy to do stuff, but that didn't matter. Her old sparkle was there, and I knew that my friend was properly back at last.

Then, at last, the weekend of Linda's wedding rolled along. Linda arrived at our house late on Thursday evening. As soon as I heard her car, I raced outside and hugged her until she begged for mercy.

'What's all that for?' she asked.

I couldn't really tell Linda the truth – that while Alice was sick, I hadn't been able to get properly excited about her wedding. I couldn't explain that now, for the first time, I was really and truly looking forward to it.

So I giggled.

'It's just fun that you're here. It's fun that there's going to be a wedding. It's fun that I got totally cool new clothes.'

Linda raised one eyebrow.

'Sheila bought you a new outfit?' she asked.

I nodded happily.

'I don't often get the opportunity for new clothes, and I couldn't waste it.'

Suddenly I noticed something.

'Where's Luka?' I asked. 'Did you forget to bring your bridegroom? You'll need him on Saturday, you know.'

She laughed.

'He's staying with my friend Laura. You can see him tomorrow. How's your mum doing?'

I rolled my eyes.

'You know Mum,' I said. 'She's taking this

catering thing *very* seriously. She's been baking since before dawn. I'm afraid to go in to the kitchen, in case I get crushed by a huge tray of sugar-free cakes or a bucket of fat-free muffins. At least I was out of the house until four o'clock. Poor Rosie wasn't so lucky – she's been hiding in her bedroom all afternoon.'

Linda laughed.

'Poor Sheila,' she said. 'But it's nice of her to go to all this trouble. Now help me with these bags, will you?'

* * *

In the morning, Mum was so busy baking that she even forgot to make my porridge. I decided to escape before she remembered.

I called for Alice so we could walk to school together.

'Linda's here,' I said. 'The wedding's going to be sooo cool – well except for the food, but who cares about that?'

Alice giggled.

'Oh, and Linda says you're to come to the wedding, since she nearly became your stepmother last year,' I added.

'That was sooo embarrassing,' she said. 'But it was kind of funny too, wasn't it?'

I nodded.

'We did some crazy things last year, didn't we?'

'Yes,' Alice agreed. 'But that was ages ago. I'm all grown up and sensible now.'

I groaned.

'You've just got better,' I said. 'Please don't go all sensible on me now. It would only make me nervous.'

Alice put on a serious face.

'Sensible Alice,' she said. 'That's going to be my new name.' Then she smiled. 'Or maybe not.'

'So, anyway, you'll come to the wedding?' I asked.

Alice grinned.

'I wouldn't miss it for anything.

*   *   *

Alice came to my house after school.

When we went in through the front door, Linda beckoned us in to the living room.

'Don't go in to the kitchen,' she whispered. 'It's crazy in there.'

'Maybe Alice should go in,' I said. 'She's brilliant at Home Ec.'

'Thanks, Meg,' said Alice, before she realised that I was joking. Then she gave me a small punch in the shoulder and pretended to be offended.

She dropped her school-bag on the floor, and threw herself on to a couch.

I turned to Linda.

'Can I show Alice your wedding dress,' I asked.

Linda nodded.

'Sure. It's in my room.'

I ran upstairs and came back down with the dress, running my fingers along the pearl trimming.

I held it up for Alice to see.

'Isn't it totally gorgeous?' I said.

Alice felt the soft fabric.

'It's beautiful,' she said. 'You're going to look like a film star, Linda.'

Linda smiled.

'Thanks, Alice,' she said, and I could see that she was really pleased.

Just then the doorbell rang. Linda peeped out through the curtains.

'It's Luka,' she said. 'Quickly hide the dress. He's not supposed to see it until tomorrow.'

I ran upstairs and hid the dress, and Linda let Luka in.

We all chatted for a while, and then Mum

appeared from the kitchen. She was wearing an apron that had once been green, but was now covered in a layer of flour. Her hair was tied up in a huge ribbon, and there was a smudge of something on her nose. She was carrying a tray heaped with funny-looking brown things.

'Who'd like a free sample?' she asked, waving the tray in the air. I wondered if this was wise. One of the brown things might suddenly make a dash for freedom.

Then I had a worse thought.

What if Luka tasted Mum's food?

Would he ring all his friends and relations and tell them not to come to the wedding?

Would they all have to cancel their flights at the last minute?

Or, even worse, would he decide it was better not to marry someone whose sister thought that these funny brown things were suitable for a wedding feast?

We couldn't let that happen. We had to make sure that Luka only tasted Mum's food when he was safely married to Linda, and it would be too late to do anything about it.

Someone had to do something.

But what?

I looked desperately at Alice and Linda. Linda was busy gazing into Luka's eyes, so she was totally useless.

Alice caught my eye, though, and I could see that she knew what I was thinking.

'No, Sheila,' she said firmly. 'We can't let you spoil the surprise. Our mouths are watering at the sight of that beautiful food, but we're going to resist. None of us is going to taste one scrap until tomorrow.'

Just then Luka dragged his eyes away from Linda's.

'You might not want some, Alice,' he said, reaching towards the tray. 'But I'm very hungry. I would like to try one please, Sheila. They look delicious.'

'So that's what they mean when they say *"Love is blind"*,' I giggled.

Mum gave me an evil look and smiled at Luka like he was the best friend she'd ever had.

Alice jumped to her feet, trying to put herself between Luka and the tray of food. As she did, though, her foot caught on the edge of the rug. Everything seemed to happen in slow motion as she stumbled forwards, knocking the tray out of Mum's hands. The tray went flying into the air and a second later, a shower of brown lumps rained down on top of us.

Alice quickly gathered them up before Luka could reach one.

'Oh, dear,' she said. 'I'm so sorry, Sheila, but these seem to be ruined.'

Mum gave a big sigh.

'Oh well,' she said. 'Don't get too upset.

There's another two hundred outside, just waiting to go in to the oven.'

Alice and I started to laugh.

'I don't really see what the joke is,' said Mum, but no one was listening.

Linda saw her opportunity.

'Come on, Luka,' she said. 'It's time you went home. You've got a big day tomorrow, and you need your beauty sleep. And besides, it's bad luck to see your bride the night before the wedding.'

Luka smiled at her.

'Every day I see you is a lucky day.'

'Aaaaah, isn't that the sweetest thing you've ever heard?' said Alice, and we all laughed again.

Chapter twenty-nine

All that evening, Mum stayed locked up in the kitchen, and the rest of us decided that it was easier to leave her there. I chatted to Linda and Alice, but soon I started to get worried.

It was the night before her wedding, and Linda was supposed to be the happiest woman in the world.

But it was clear that she wasn't.

After a while, she pulled a huge bar of chocolate out of her bag, and shared it around, but it wasn't like it was supposed to be. She didn't look like she was enjoying the chocolate.

She didn't even look

like she was enjoying breaking Mum's stupid food rules.

As the evening went on, Linda got quieter and quieter. She stopped laughing at Alice's jokes (even the funny ones), and she looked like someone who was preparing for a funeral instead of a wedding.

Suddenly she stood up.

'I can't go through with this,' she said.

I hurried over and put my arm around her.

'Don't worry,' I said. 'Mum's food isn't that bad really. And everyone will be so busy talking about how beautiful your dress is, they won't notice anyway. And besides, even if the food isn't nice, at least you know it will be healthy.'

Alice joined in to help me.

'And the people from Latvia might think that all food in Ireland is like this.'

Linda made a face.

'I'm not talking about the *food*,' she said. 'I'm

talking about the *wedding*. I don't think I can go through with it.'

There was a very long silence.

At last Alice spoke.

'Don't you love Luka?' she asked bravely.

Even the mention of his name made Linda smile.

'I do love him,' she said. 'I love him more than I've ever loved anyone.'

'Er … so where's the problem?' I asked.

Linda gave a big long sigh.

'It's just too much,' she said. 'I'm afraid. I'm afraid I won't be a good enough wife for Luka. I'm afraid of the fuss tomorrow. I'm afraid … well I'm afraid of everything. It's too big a step. I can't go through with it.'

Alice spoke firmly, 'It's just pre-wedding nerves. Remember Louise said that happened to her cousin the night before her wedding too?'

I nodded my head, even though I couldn't

remember Louise saying anything like that.

Linda looked at us sadly.

'Thanks, girls,' she said, 'but I know it's not that. It's just … well it's all too much. I'm afraid we're going to have to tell everyone that the wedding is off.'

As she spoke she pulled her mobile phone out of her pocket.

'I suppose I'll have to talk to Luka first,' she said, pressing some buttons on the phone.

She held the phone to her ear, and then clicked it off.

'It's useless. There's a really bad mobile phone signal in Laura's house, and she hasn't got a land-line. I'll just have to go over there.'

There had been a constant clattering of pots and pans in the background all evening, but now it suddenly got louder. There was a crash, and then Mum said the rudest word I'd ever heard her say. I looked towards the kitchen.

'Bags not being the one who has to tell Mum that the wedding's off,' I said.

Linda suddenly went pale. She took a step towards the door.

'I might as well make a start,' she said. 'I'll tell Sheila, then I'll go and tell Luka, and then we'd better start ringing all of our friends. Luka's family are already on their way. He'll have to go to the airport and tell them they've had a wasted journey.'

Suddenly Alice stepped between Linda and the kitchen door, skidding as she stepped on a brown lumpy thing that we'd missed earlier.

'No,' she said as she recovered her balance. 'Don't tell Sheila. She'll go crazy.'

Linda nodded sadly.

'I know she'll go crazy, so I'd better get it over with.'

'No,' said Alice. 'Don't do anything foolish. Just give me a minute to think.'

Linda and I sat down, and watched Alice for a while. She was busy picking brown stuff from the sole of her shoe.

At last she spoke.

'OK, Linda,' she said. 'What do you think will happen when you go to see Luka?'

Linda thought for a minute. She was pale, and I could see that she was close to tears.

'He'll be sad,' she said. 'But then he'll be like you. He'll say it's just nerves. He'll try to change my mind.'

'And do you want that to happen?'

Linda shook her head.

'Well, no ... or ... yes ... or I don't know. Well, I want to change my mind, but I won't – no matter what he says. So we'll just have a big fight, and I don't want that. In time, Luka will understand why I'm doing this, but if I see him tonight, I know it will end in tears.'

Alice gave a small smile.

'That's the most important thing settled, so. Now, what do you think will happen when you tell Sheila?'

Linda sighed.

'Like I said, she'll go crazy. She's worked so hard, and she hates to see food wasted. And she'll probably feel bad for Luka and his family, and all the guests who've come all the way …'

Alice smiled again. Why did she suddenly see so much to smile about?

'Now, last question. What do you think will happen when you tell all of your friends?'

Linda gave an even bigger sigh.

'I can't even think that far ahead. It's going to take the whole night. Some of them are travelling already, and I don't have all of their mobile numbers. And the ones I do manage to talk to …… how on earth am I going to explain so many times? And what's Luka going to say to his parents? Oh girls, how am I going to manage this?'

Alice folded her arms.

'Right then, this is what we do. We say nothing to Sheila. We say nothing to any of the other guests either. We just all go to the registry office at eleven o'clock, like you're supposed to—'

'But—', began Linda.

'Don't interrupt,' said Alice. 'When you get to the registry office, everyone will be together, so you'll only have to explain once. One simple explanation, and everything is sorted.'

Linda shook her head.

'But I can't do that to Luka. None of this is his fault. How can I embarrass him in front of everyone?'

Now Alice smiled again.

'You won't embarrass Luka, because he won't be there. In a few minutes I'll go over and tell him what's happened. I'll tell him that you'll meet him somewhere else at eleven thirty tomorrow, and that you'll explain properly then.'

'But he'll be upset,' protested Linda.

'Of course he'll be upset, but it'll be fine. Trust me. I'll tell him not to worry. I'll tell him you still love him. I'm sure he'll understand.'

Linda looked at me.

'What do you think, Megan?' she asked.

'Alice can be very persuasive,' I said. 'If anyone can make Luka understand, she can.'

Linda looked at Alice again.

'But what about all this food?'

Alice grinned.

'You know Sheila would prefer to see the food eaten, and all those people are going to be hungry, so they might as well come back here anyway. It'll be just like a wedding – except without a bride and groom. And you and Luka can go off for lunch somewhere, and forget about all the fuss back here.'

Linda still looked doubtful.

'I don't know,' she said.

Alice sighed.

'Do you have any better ideas?'

Linda shook her head slowly.

'That's it then,' said Alice standing up. 'You can leave everything to me.'

Suddenly I felt guilty. I sooo didn't want to be caught up in this scene with Luka, but after all, Linda was my aunt. How could I let Alice handle all the bad stuff on her own?

'Er … should I go with you?' I said to Alice.

Alice shook her head.

'No. Someone needs to stay here with Linda.'

Then she headed for the door.

'Wait,' said Linda. 'Megan, can you get me paper and an envelope? I think I'll write a letter to Luka. You know … explaining how I feel.'

I didn't know if that was a good idea, but I went and got what Linda needed. Then Alice and I stood back, while Linda spent *ages* writing a letter. She then put the letter in the envelope, sealed it, kissed it and handed it to Alice.

Alice took it like it was the most precious thing in the world. Then she went to the door again. Just before she went out, she turned back and smiled at Linda.

'Don't worry,' she said. 'Everything will turn out fine. You just wait and see.'

*   *   *

Half an hour later, Alice was back. Mum was still in the kitchen, and Dad and Rosie were doing jigsaws in Rosie's bedroom.

'Well?' I asked Alice.

'What did Luka say?' asked Linda at the same time.

'It was all fine,' said Alice breezily. 'He was a bit upset, but after he read your letter, I think he understood how you feel.'

'I should go to see him,' said Linda.

'No,' said Alice.

'Or I could try ringing him one more time.'

'No,' said Alice again. 'And I told him not to ring you either. Trust me, it's better this way. You tell everyone tomorrow, and then you and Luka can have a lovely afternoon together. That'll be the messy stuff over, and then you can live happily ever after. Now I've got to go. I'll call over in the morning, OK?'

I nodded.

Suddenly I felt like we were making a very big mistake.

Alice has always loved plotting and scheming, but surely this was too big, even for her?

This wasn't fun and games. This was a *wedding*. These were two lives that she was meddling in.

But who else could I ask for advice?

If I went to Dad, he'd just say to ask Mum.

If I asked Mum she'd probably have a heart attack at any hint that the wedding might not go ahead.

And Linda was too nervous to be of any use to anyone.

Linda was twisting her engagement ring on her finger.

Should I ask her if I could borrow it?

Maybe I could use it to make one more wish?

Then I decided that was a really bad idea. Wishing on Linda's ring had got me into enough trouble already.

So all I could do was give Linda a hug good night, and go off to my room to worry in peace.

Chapter thirty

In the morning I got up and put on my old jeans and a sweatshirt. Then I realised that this was a big mistake. I had to pretend that I thought I was going to a wedding. And besides, if mum got any idea that there wasn't going to be a wedding, she'd want to bring my new clothes back to the shop. If I wore them first, she couldn't do that.

So I took out the cool new skinny jeans, and

the beautiful green top and the pumps. I ripped the tags off everything, and put them all on.

Then I went downstairs. Once again, Mum was in the kitchen.

She looked up when I came in.

'You look lovely, Megan,' she said.

'Thanks, Mum,' I said. 'You look … er … busy.'

'I'll never be finished in time,' she moaned. 'The wedding is going to be a disaster, and it's all going to be my fault.'

What would she say if she knew what I knew?

The wedding was going to be a disaster all right, but for once, my mum's food was going to have nothing to do with it.

Suddenly I felt sorry for her.

'Do you want me to help you?' I asked.

She shook her head.

'Thanks, love, but no. You go keep Linda company. I think she's a bit nervous. Tell her we have to leave in half an hour.'

I went in to the other room. Rosie and Dad were there, all dressed in their best clothes. Linda was in an old track-suit of Mum's.

'Linda,' I hissed. 'You need to go and get ready.'

She gave me a funny look, which I ignored. I took her by the arm and dragged her up the stairs.

'What's the point in getting dressed up?' she said.

I sighed.

'Use your head. I know Mum is obsessed with chickpea pancakes right now, but even she will notice that there's something wrong if you go to the registry office looking like that. And you don't want a scene before we even get there, do you?'

Linda slapped her forehead.

'You're right,' she said. 'I'm so nervous, I'm

not thinking straight.'

I hugged her.

'Don't worry,' I said. 'The worst part will be telling everyone. After that you'll be fine. Now quickly, jump in to the shower.'

By the time Linda was showered and dressed, Alice had called over, looking totally cool in a new skirt and top.

(I was so glad to see her happy again that I forgave her for looking better than me.)

Alice and I helped Linda to blow-dry her hair, and then Alice insisted on making Linda up with some of the make-up she'd bought for her wedding day.

'It's going to be a long day,' she said. 'And you'll feel better if you look your best.'

Linda didn't even argue. She was quiet and obedient and sad-looking.

Just as Linda was ready, a very frazzled-looking Mum put her head around the door.

'Everyone ready?' she asked.

We all nodded.

Mum had showered and put on the nice dress she'd had for my Confirmation, but the red on her cheeks betrayed the work she'd been doing all morning.

'You look lovely, Mum,' I said, and the lie was worth it for the happy smile she gave me.

And then Linda, Mum, Dad, Rosie, Alice and I all set off for the wedding that wasn't meant to be.

Chapter thirty-one

As we got closer to the registry office, Linda began to slow her steps. Alice and I slowed down too, letting Mum, Dad and Rosie walk ahead.

'I can't go through with this,' said Linda. 'I'm too much of a coward. I'm not brave enough to get married, and I'm not brave enough to tell people that I'm not brave enough to get married. Someone else will have to do it. Sheila....' she suddenly called.

Mum stopped

walking and looked back.

'What is it?' she asked.

Alice made a furious face at Linda and then smiled at Mum.

'Linda was just going to thank you for all your hard work,' she said, squeezing Linda's arm tightly, 'weren't you, Linda?'

Linda nodded.

'Er … yes. That's it. Thanks, Sheila.'

Mum gave her a funny look.

'You're welcome,' she said. 'Now let's keep going, or we're going to be late.'

*　　*　　*

I wished the walk would go on forever, as I sooo did not want to get to the registry office.

I soooo did not want to be part of what was going to happen next.

Still, even though we walked really slowly, we soon turned the last corner, and found ourselves right outside the office, where crowds of people in their best clothes were milling around.

'This is awful,' said Linda. 'I have to get it over with as quickly as possible.'

Then, before Alice and I could do anything, Linda broke away from us. She ran up to the first group of people – three old women in flowery hats.

'Linda!' said one of them, 'your dress is simply—'

Before she could finish her sentence, Linda interrupted her, 'Can you just go inside quickly please?' she said. 'I'll explain everything once everyone is together.'

They gave her puzzled looks, but obediently walked towards the door of the registry office. Then, as the crowd parted, I gulped.

There was Luka.

He was walking towards us.

He was wearing a beautiful suit, with a flower

in the lapel.

He had a huge smile on his face.

I looked quickly at Alice.

'He ignored you,' I whispered. 'He came anyway.'

Alice didn't answer.

I looked at Linda. She looked like she'd seen a ghost.

Luka raised his hands in the air.

'My beautiful bride,' he said loudly, and everyone cheered as he put his arms around Linda. He twirled her around in the air until all we could see was the rush of soft blue silk, spinning in the air like a giant windmill.

At last Luka put Linda down.

'Come on, my darling,' he said. 'Let's go inside and get married.'

Linda gasped as she tried to catch her breath. Her face was pink and her hair was tossed, but she was beaming.

She leaned towards Alice.

'What's going on?' she whispered.

Alice shrugged.

'Do you want to get married?'

Linda nodded, still with a huge smile on her face.

'Yes, more than anything in the world.'

'Well then,' said Alice. 'Isn't it lucky that I forgot to go and see Luka last night?'

'I don't understand,' said Linda.

Alice shrugged.

'I've been around a lot,' she said, sounding like an old woman. 'I knew you were only suffering from last-minute nerves. I couldn't just stand by and watch you make a total mess of your wedding day.'

Linda put her hand to her face.

'But what about the letter I wrote to Luka?'

Alice grinned as she took the still-sealed letter out of her pocket and slipped it into

Linda's handbag.

'You can show it to your grandchildren,' she said. 'Now hurry up. Your bridegroom is waiting.'

I turned to Alice.

'You're incredible,' I said.

Alice grinned.

'I know,' she said. 'Now let's go inside. I've invested a lot in this wedding. I want to be sure to get a good view.'

Chapter thirty-two

An hour later we were back at the house. Mum and Dad, who don't speak Latvian, were trying to chat with Luka's parents, who don't speak English. There was lots of smiling and nodding and waving of hands, but I don't think much information was being exchanged.

Luka, who speaks both languages, wasn't much help. He and Linda were sitting on the couch.

They were holding hands like a couple in a soppy movie, and they were both smiling like they never wanted to stop.

I watched as the three old women in flowery hats went up to Linda.

'Outside the registry office,' one of them said, 'you wanted to tell us something.'

Linda's face went red.

'Oh,' she said. 'That was—'

Alice raced over.

'She wanted to tell you where the fire exits were, and then she forgot. Isn't it lucky there wasn't a fire, or we could all have been killed?'

The three women nodded their heads, making their hats bob up and down like a field full of flowers in the wind.

'Thanks, Alice,' mouthed Linda, and Alice smiled.

'Any time,' she said.

* * *

Shortly afterwards Mum disappeared in to the kitchen. Half an hour later, she announced that the food was ready, and everyone crowded around the table.

Even I had to admit that the food smelled lovely, and I was glad to see that people seemed to be enjoying it.

So many people congratulated Mum that she began to be embarrassed.

'It's nothing,' she said. 'Just a few things I threw together this morning.'

Alice and I looked at Linda and we all laughed.

When everyone else was served, Alice and I got plates and went to the table. Just then there was a ring at the door.

Alice followed me into the hall. I opened the front door to see a pizza delivery man on the door step. He was carrying a pizza box, with two cans of fizzy drinks balanced on top. I could smell yummy cheese and onions and pepperoni.

I could almost taste the fizzy bubbles of the drink on the back of my throat.

'Sorry,' I said sadly. 'We didn't order pizza. I think you must have the wrong house.'

The man looked at the label on the box.

'I don't think so,' he said. 'The address looks right.'

I sighed, wondering which one of our lucky neighbours was having pizza for lunch.

'What name is on the order?' I asked.

The man read the label.

'It says *for Megan and Alice*,' he said. 'That wouldn't be you two, would it?'

Alice and I looked at each other. Alice grinned.

'If it's a pizza, and it's got our names on it, I ain't arguing,' she said.

Suddenly Linda was behind us. She took the pizza and the drinks, paid the man and closed the door behind him.

She held the pizza towards Alice and me. I

took it quickly, just in case she changed her mind.

'My treat,' said Linda. 'And thank you, Alice. Thank you very, very much. You will never know what a big favour you did me yesterday.'

Then she gave Alice a big hug.

'Maybe you'd better eat that in your room, Megan,' she said. 'We can't have the other guests getting jealous, can we?'

And then she went back to her husband and her party.

*   *   *

Twenty minutes later, Alice and I were lying on my bed, licking our lips. The empty drink cans were on the locker beside my bed. The empty pizza box lay on the floor, and Domino was licking the last traces of food from the cardboard.

'Should we go back to the party?' asked Alice.

'In a minute,' I said lazily. It was nice lying

there with Alice, talking about nothing much.

'You shouldn't really be here,' I said after a while. 'You should be in France now – in your boarding school.'

Suddenly I had an amazing thought.

'No one else would have been brave enough to do what you did. If you weren't here, Linda would have gone ahead and cancelled her wedding.'

Alice smiled.

'Yeah, she would have, wouldn't she? So I suppose it's lucky I fell.'

'It's lucky that Domino got stuck in the tree,' I said.

'It's lucky that of all the houses on this road, Domino chose this one to stray into last year.'

I leaned over and stroked Domino.

'So black cats are lucky after all,' I said to her. 'You saved Linda's wedding.'

Domino didn't seem impressed. She licked her lips and then jumped on to the windowsill.

'And if you get caught up any more trees, I'm not rescuing you,' said Alice. 'You're on your own.'

Domino just gave her one of her sly stares, and then she jumped out through the open window.

I turned to Alice.

'Thanks for saving Domino,' I said. 'And thanks for saving Linda. And I'm really, really sorry about France.'

Alice smiled.

'That's OK. And don't worry about France. I'm over it. And remember Megan, no matter what happens, there's always something else nice waiting around the corner.'

I smiled. Maybe she was right. Maybe there always was something nice waiting around the corner.

Then my best friend and I got up and went back to the party.

THE 'ALICE & MEGAN' SERIES
BY

Judi Curtin

HAVE YOU READ THEM ALL?

Don't miss all the great books about
Alice & Megan:

Alice Next Door
Alice Again
Don't Ask Alice
Alice in the Middle
Bonjour Alice
Alice & Megan Forever
Alice to the Rescue
Alice & Megan's Cookbook
Available from all good bookshops

Best friends NEED to be together. Don't they?

Poor Megan! Not alone is she stuck with totally uncool parents, and a little sister who is too cute for words, but now her best friend, Alice, has moved away. Now Megan has to go to school and face the dreaded Melissa all on her own.

The two friends hatch a risky plot to get back together. But can their secret plan work?

It's mid-term break and Megan's off to visit Alice.

Megan is hoping for a nice trouble-free few days with her best friend. No such luck! She soon discovers that Alice is once again plotting and scheming. It seems that Alice's mum Veronica has a new boyfriend. The plan is to discover who he is, and to get rid of him!

Alice and Megan are together again!

They are both looking forward to their Confirmation, especially as their two families are going out to dinner together to celebrate.
But not even a meal can be simple when Alice is around as she decides to hatch a plan to get her parents back together ...

Alice in the Middle

Judi Curtin

Best friends forever?

Megan can't wait to go away
to Summer Camp with Alice!
It will be fantastic — no organic porridge, no school,
nothing but fun! But when Alice makes friends with
Hazel, Megan begins to feel left out. Hazel's pretty,
sophisticated and popular, and Alice seems to think
she's amazing.
Is Megan going to lose her very best friend?

Sunshine & yummy French food — sounds like the perfect holiday!

Megan's really looking forward to the summer holidays — her whole family is going to France, and best of all Alice is coming too! But when Alice tries to make friends with a local French boy things begin to get very interesting ...

Alice and Megan are starting secondary school.

New subjects, new teachers and new friends — it's going to take a bit of getting used to. And when Megan meets Marcus, the class bad-boy who's always in trouble, but doesn't seem to care, things really start to get complicated.
At least she has Home Ec class with Alice — the worst cook in the school — to look forward to, so school's not all bad!

Get cooking with Alice & Megan!

Alice and Megan are writing a cook-book. But Alice is not the world's the greatest cook, so could it be a recipe for disaster? Well, not with Megan's help .... This fun-filled cookbook is packed with brilliant recipes. Why not wake up to French toast and tropical smoothies? Or go to school with raspberry muffins and pasta salad? Or snack on s'mores and quesadillas? Or impress your friends with home-made burgers followed by ice cream with toffee sauce? All this and more included!

Brilliant Breakfasts . Lucky Lunchboxes . Super Snacks . Marvellous Main Courses . Delicious Desserts . Cakes & Cookies.

MEET GREAT NEW CHARACTERS FROM

Judi Curtin

Eva is the girl with everything — great birthday parties, a luxury home, designer clothes and manicured nails — until her world is turned upside down. Forced to move house and school when her dad loses his job, Eva thinks life is over. But, with the help of some new friends and the mysterious Madame Margarita, she finds out that there's more to life than shopping.

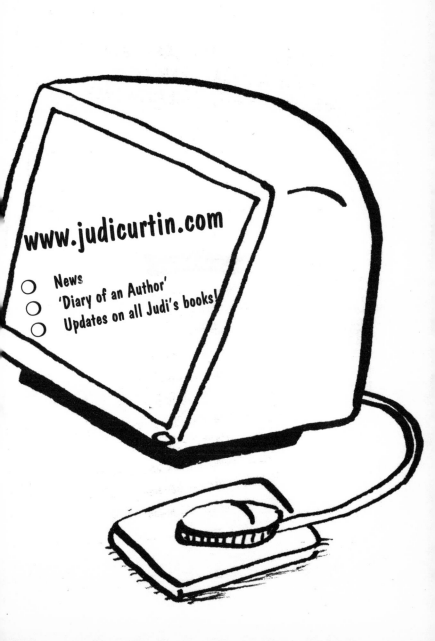